Are Y

Are You She?

edited by
Lesley Glaister

**Tindal
Street
Press**

First published in 2004 by
Tindal Street Press Ltd.
217 The Custard Factory, Gibb Street, Birmingham B9 4AA
www.tindalstreet.co.uk

Photos of Myra Connell, Mandy Sutter and Polly Wright
© Mark Johnson (www.mjohnsonphotography.com).
Photo of Sidura Ludwig © Jason Shron.
Photos of Mandy Sutter and Myra Connell used by
kind permission of Birmingham Museum and Art Gallery.
Photo of Polly Wright used by kind permission of the Ikon Gallery.

A CIP catalogue reference for this book is available from
the British Library.

ISBN 0 9541303 9 1

Typeset by Country Setting, Kingsdown, Kent.
Printed and bound in Great Britain by Clays Ltd, St Ives PLC

Contents

Introduction

One of my favourite occupations is to dawdle along a street at dusk, just as the lights come on but before the curtains are drawn. This is not from any particularly voyeuristic streak but for the tantalizing glimpses of other lives – teasing, intriguing, suggestive of so much more. And it is with a similar pleasure that I pick up a collection of short stories by new writers, wondering what glimpses of life they will give me, what they will have lit up within their frames.

Short stories are not something I'd choose to read instead of novels – I always have at least one of those on the go – but they are something I like to read alongside novels because the two narrative forms offer such different pleasures. When reading a novel I often want to become engrossed, to lose myself – in other words to indulge in a form of escapism – but when reading a short story, I want not so much to escape from life as to engage with it.

Because of this quality of engagement, I think, short stories require a different and more attentive kind of reading. I find it is best not to gorge on too many at once, but to read one at a time and allow it the space to settle in the imagination. A slim volume such as this one, which gives a taster of the work of just four writers, allows each story the space for the kind of considered reading it deserves.

*

'Hero' by Myra Connell is a brave and bold story, a double first-person narrative that takes us straight to the heart of a moment of recent history – the aftermath of 11 September 2001. A mother looks on helplessly as her son, the lone survivor of his team of fire fighters, is engaged in the awful work of searching the rubble for human remains. It centres on his discovery of a human arm. 'It had fallen palm down and I could see the two small diamonds on the ring, and the nails had been painted, not loud and bright, but gentle, just a shine and the whole thing dirty and scratched and bloodstained now.' The power of this story lies in the way the severed arm becomes a symbol of the vast human waste. Its tone is admirably controlled and understated, delivering to the reader something of the numbness and even eventual banality of the tragedy.

Myra's other story, 'Heidi's House', is a quieter domestic tale that explores the unease experienced by a woman staying in the house of a stranger – while Mandy Sutter's 'The Therapist' reverses this effect. Here an elderly woman is challenged by the unsettling experience of witnessing a stream of strangers entering her own home.

Set in Nigeria, 'Lasiren' – Mandy's other contribution – demonstrates within itself the power of story. A seven-year-old child is told by a family servant about the mermaid – Lasiren – and willingly suspends her disbelief in order to overcome her fear of water. The tone of this story captures something of the magic and bewilderment of a child's perceptions yet allows 'a glimmer of fear, a shiny edge' to glint through the fabric of the prose.

Both Polly Wright's stories are concerned with the peculiar intensity of mother-daughter relationships. In 'Finding Alteration' the newly divorced Ruth hankers after her youth and becomes aware of the contrast between her daughter's burgeoning sexuality and her own middle age. The furious mixture of neediness and near revulsion as a daughter contemplates her mother's sexuality is painfully conveyed. A similar intensity is echoed in 'Shropshire Gold' – though with the irony that the middle-aged narrator is stuck in a sort of perpetual adolescence, arrested in her development by regret for a daughter she never had.

Sidura Ludwig's two connected stories are set in Canada and have the easy, colloquial tone that many British writers envy their transatlantic colleagues. 'Ten Ways to Better Customer Relations' is a quirky love story that relates the meeting of Cathy, a widow, with David, the husband of a dementia sufferer. 'Interlake Evergreens' takes us deeper into their lives and explores in a subtle and moving way the difficult joy of finding love at this time of life and the pain of letting go of the past.

From a wide variety of settings and subjects these writers tackle the shared themes of love, loss and learning. They bring to each story a freshness of voice and a perceptiveness that makes each glow seductively from its frame. This is a very superior streetful of glimpses that I feel sure will leave readers engaged, intrigued, moved, amused and imaginatively stirred.

Lesley Glaister
August 2004

Mandy Sutter

MANDY SUTTER is a poet and short story writer; her poetry collections *Permission to Stare* and *Game* were published in the 1990s. Her forthcoming novel *The Habit of Loneliness* is set in Leeds, Scarborough and Nigeria, where she grew up in the 1960s during the days of oil exploration.

Lasiren

Mandy Sutter

Ever since they came to Nigeria a year ago, Maureen has made fruitless attempts to coax Sarah into the club swimming pool. She stands waist deep in the turquoise cube.

– Come on, darling. The water won't bite you!

But she is wearing a scary white rubber hat covered in white rubber flowers that makes her face look too big. And there are other children in the water whose loud enjoyment intimidates Sarah. As do the young men who swim so fast, up and down, up and down.

And it's not just the pool. Before they left England, Gran told her the story of her own near death by drowning. As she made up the fire one winter evening, rolling sheets of the *Gloucester Citizen* diagonally, twisting them into springy sticks and pressing them into the grate, Gran told Sarah that as an infant she was 'somehow' dropped over the side of a ferry. All was well that ended well. She was 'borne up on her swaddling clothes' and came to no harm. But years later, Gran said, as she held a double sheet over the mouth of the fireplace to draw the fire until everything behind the paper was orange and roaring, a gypsy woman told her that she would die by drowning. And since that day she has refused to travel anywhere by water.

While Sarah's mother joked about Gran being afraid even to step across puddles; while Sarah's father gave a rendition of 'Doctor Foster went to Gloucester'; while a hole appeared suddenly in the paper, its burnt edges travelling rapidly outwards until Gran thrust it into the grate, seeming to put her bent fingers right into the fire; Sarah, who was five and had seen a ferry, conjured unbearable contrasts in her mind.

The pale baby: the black, churning waters. The pale, tiny baby: the long, long drop down the steep sides of the ferry. The pale, tiny, warm baby: the plunge into the freezing, terrible cold.

Those things were bad enough. Yet something worried her even more. How could a baby 'somehow' get dropped over the side of a ferry?

Now, every time Sarah sits on the edge of the pool, thinking *this time I'll do it*, Gran's story bobs into her mind and won't be pushed back under.

Her mother becomes exasperated. One day she loses her temper.

– For goodness' sake, Sarah! I just don't know how to help you!

But it turns out someone else does.

Her parents have a servant they call Richard. And on one of their customary holiday breaks, which involve packing up the Chevrolet and heading out of Aba Town for a few days at the coast forty miles away, they take Richard with them.

From the start, Richard makes things more fun. He's used to riding in mammy-wagons, the slow dilapidated buses the locals use, not cars. He's used to hanging off the roof or riding shotgun at the back, not sitting inside. He perches on the edge of his seat and, as the car bumps over potholes in the dirt road and swerves to avoid suicidal bullfrogs, he keeps banging his head on the roof. Maureen tells him to sit back in his seat, but he only obliges her briefly. He forgets his deferential manners and laughs and shrieks and says things in Ibo that sound like swearing. Sarah, up front between her parents, sneaks envious looks round into the back.

They arrive in the early evening, their hair thick with the dust that's blown in off the road. It's bliss to get out of the car at last and feel the air on the backs of her legs, which were swimming in sweat on the seat. Her skirt, sodden but cooling rapidly in the evening air, clings to her legs. She runs to the toilet. Her father never stops on the way. He says a bunch of natives could spring out of nowhere in a matter of seconds and swarm the car. He says they're in the sixties now, and there's something on called a General Strike that's making people do bad things to each other.

They're staying on the beach, in huts made of mud and cane with thatched pointed roofs. The sand is fabulous, soft and white and deep.

And the place is full of monkeys. They swing about in the trees that fringe the beach and cluster in chatty, screeching groups. Sarah doesn't quite know how she feels about the monkeys. In one way they're cuddly, with their fur and their funny little faces, but in another they're scary, like the group of children at school who seemed to run the playground.

They pinch anything you leave outside for more than five minutes. Or even things on view inside an open window. A teddy bear, the spare keys, the cardboard tube from inside a toilet roll: it doesn't matter to them. Everything is treated just the same – explored, then divided down to its most basic parts. Like doing sums at school. Then they throw the parts back at you, aiming for your head.

*

Richard unloads the bags from the boot. Her mother feels Sarah's forehead and tuts.

– You're very hot. What about a dip in the sea?

Sarah swallows. The more no one acknowledges her fear, the worse it gets.

She stares at the mass of water that creeps up and down the beach, roaring softly like an animal.

– I don't feel like it. I've got a headache.

Her mother sighs. – Come on, Sarah. You're a big girl now. Big girls aren't afraid of the sea.

She goes off into the hut. Sarah holds in the tears like she held her wee on the journey. Swimming is something everyone can do, except her.

Richard notices. He comes over and crouches before her, barefoot as usual in drooping khaki shorts. He always has a smile for her and now that smile makes her tears brim over. To catch them, he presses his thumb gently to the skin beneath her eyes. His thumb feels rough, but nice.

– Hey, child. Why you not wan' go?

His attention makes her feel even more ashamed. She looks down and a tear makes a tiny damp pinprick in the sand.

– Hey! Me frighten too.

She makes a face. He's not the kind of person who gets scared. She saw him only yesterday climbing on top of the roof without a ladder to fix something. But his face is serious.

– When me same age as you, me mama throw me in river to make me strong. But it make me frighten.

Sarah blinks.

– We go in water together. We help one another. If you come in water with me, me not so frighten.

Sarah looks at him suspiciously. But his face is thoughtful.

– Now I help you mamafadder with bags. Now, you think about what I am say. You go look at sea and talk to Lasiren. You make friend.

– Who?

Richard points out to sea. But Sarah can see no friend, just the brownish heave of waves. The sea's hands, reaching up the sand towards her.

– Lasiren. The spirit of the sea. She is white woman, like you mama. But her hair not black, like you mama. It yellow. And where you got two legs, she got big tail. Shiny fish tail.

Sarah smiles. Now she knows what he's talking about.

– Oh, you mean a *mermaid*.

Richard nods. – OK, mer-maid. Lasiren. You know what she charm is?

– Charm?

– Yes. She lucky sign.

Sarah knows about mermaids. Has heard enough stories to know that what mermaids do all day is sit about on rocks combing their long hair.

– I know. It's a hairbrush and mirror.

Richard gives a shout of laughter. – You plenty clever, child! The mirror, yes, that's she charm!

Often when Richard laughs, water springs down his cheeks, and he has to wipe it away. Sarah gazes up at him hopefully. But their conversation is interrupted.

Maureen shouts from the hut doorway. – Richard! We want everything unpacked before supper.

– I come, Madam.

He bends down again to Sarah.

– Lasiren. One more sign she have. What she got stuck round that mirror and that hairbrush? For to look pretty?

Sarah grins. – I know! Shells! Seashells!

Richard beams. – You see! How can a young girl who know so much about she sea spirit, how can that plenty clever girl be frighten?

While the adults get on with things in the house, Sarah goes carefully down to the sea and stands just out of reach of the waves, fighting the urge to scream and run every time a big wave comes up the beach, trying to snatch her in. Was Lasiren a good spirit? What if she decided she needed trainee mermaids, and took Sarah down to live at the bottom of the sea?

Sarah wanders slowly along the tide-line. There are shells here and there, half submerged, but when she bends to pick them up, rubbing the damp grains away, they are ordinary. She decides to find a shell for Lasiren. But it will need to be a proper one – a big spiral shell maybe with mother of pearl inside, or one of those thick ridged fans like the sign for petrol. Shell petrol.

She wanders on, glancing back at the huts to make sure no one's calling for her. Her father has walked down to the edge of the sea. He's also in khaki shorts, but wears socks and sandals. He sees her and they wave. His wave gives her a burst of energy and she runs till she's level with the monkey trees. The monkeys roam freely, but there's a clump of trees they favour.

The last time she was there, a particularly bold monkey jumped on her back and pulled her hair slide right off her head. It was so sudden – a thump in the back, a sharp smell and a hard yank on her hair. She screamed, and the monkey shot off across the sand and up the nearest tree. She decided not to cry, but stood staring up at the monkey turning the bright pink clip with its little bunch of fake red cherries over and over in its hand scornfully, as if thinking it had made a serious fashion mistake.

Now, under the monkey trees she sees colours, bits of things dotted in the sand. She wonders whether her hair slide might be among them. Feeling the top of her head to make sure she's got no slides in today, she heads away from the sea, up into the more hummocky sand towards the trees. She's out of sight of the huts now. Nearing the trees, she treads carefully, knowing that the ground is probably also dotted with all that comes out of monkeys' bottoms.

She can see a small group of them in the treetops half-way to the sky. Sarah steals nervous glances upwards but they don't seem too bothered about her.

Under the trees is a trove of broken treasures. A tinted lens from someone's sunglasses winking up from the grassy sand. She picks it up. It's dented all over with tiny teeth-marks. An undeveloped film, snaking over the sand. She moves further into the trees. A black disc that looks like a bit of camera. Three teaspoons, bent and poking up out of the sand at different angles. The monkeys yell above her.

A few steps on, there's a cover from a book, a picture of a man in front of a blackboard pointing at sums. *Times Tables for African Schools*. Then a few steps more, a scattering of strange shiny things, small and smooth, like metal monkey droppings. She scoops two of them up and weighs them in her hand. They're heavy.

And then, half buried by the base of one of the trees, what looks like a large glass marble. She picks it up. There's something sticky on it that makes the sand cling to it in patterns, like a globe of the world. She rubs at the sand. There's colour underneath, blue and white, like the centre of a marble. She will have to take it down to the sea, to wash it.

Then her eye catches something by the base of one of the trees, something pink. Perhaps this is her hair slide. She slips the metal things and the glass ball into her pocket. She moves hopefully towards the tree. What she sees makes her forget her hair slide instantly. It's a big spiral shell, bigger than any she has seen on the beach, as big as half her hand. She picks it up, feeling the outside, white and rough as chalk. She turns it over to examine the inside. She sees a satiny-smooth pink path, leading from the shell's lip inwards. She pokes her finger into it, knowing her finger is too fat. She tries to peer down it, but her eye can get no further than her finger. It's beautiful. Just the right sort of thing for a mermaid.

Back at the huts, Richard's shout makes her heart swell with pride.

– You find plenty good shell! You smart girl!

He comes up for a closer look.

– Is for Lasiren?

She nods, looks up at him shyly.

– You find such plenty good shell, Lasiren let we swim all the way to England, return ticket!

He takes the shell from her and strokes it just as she did, then pokes his finger inside pointlessly, just as she did.

– Wait till I show Mummy!

He looks thoughtful. – Listen. Show you mama you shell is fine. But you no speak of Lasiren. We make big surprise when we show you mama you no frighten no more. Then we tell. OK?

Sarah nods gleefully at the idea.

– Can we go to meet Lasiren now? Can we?

He crouches down beside her. – You mama, she want you for to eat soup now. And you mama is right. You need full belly for to meet with Lasiren. Go. We talk after.

They eat their supper around a clumsy raffia-work table that makes their glasses wobble and spill on the dirt floor.

– Mummy. Have you ever seen a mermaid, here in Nigeria? Are they the same as English ones?

Maureen smiles. – They might look a bit different from English ones. Eat up now. You've only had about half.

– I don't really like yam.

– But try and eat the meat. Meat's good for mermaids. It makes their hair grow thick and long and dark.

– But mermaids have all got blonde hair, haven't they? Richard said.

Her father laughs. – I suppose they're all white, too?

Sarah looks at him anxiously. He smiles and puts his hand on her shoulder.

– Just kidding you. Of course they are. Find anything interesting by the monkey trees? Those little devils will pinch anything.

From the pocket of her dress, she pulls out the metal droppings and the glass marble. The sand has rubbed off the marble. Inside, you can see a sphere of dull white with a small ring of blue inside it, then a central spot of black, like a bull's eye. She puts it on the table and it rolls slowly across the tilted, uneven surface towards her mother.

Maureen screams and jumps from the table, sending her soup bowl to the dirt floor.

Her father gets to his feet more slowly. He stares in disbelief at the glass ball.

– For God's sake! That's some poor bugger's glass eye! And those are bullets – live ones by the look of it!

He scoops the offending objects from the table and goes out. Richard clears up the spilt soup and fetches Maureen a fresh plate. Maureen sits, fanning herself with her hand. Sarah sits with her own wrongness.

Later in bed, she hears them through the cane wall. They are trying to keep their voices down, but odd words break through. She catches 'danger' and 'hotheads'. She doesn't want to hear any more, in case some of it's about her. She presses one ear to the mattress; covers the other with her pillow. She doesn't want to know who her parents are when she's not there.

She must have dozed. Her eyes snap open. Someone is whispering. She looks around her. She is alone, but the room is amazingly light – the moon shines in through the gaps in the weave, casting a colourless light, so that everything is like those old photos of Gran's. She hears her name. It's coming through the gaps too, in a squeaky whisper.

– Sarah, Miss Sarah . . .

– Richard!

– No, Miss Sarah. Richard? Who is Richard? I know no such man. I am the spirit of the sea. I am Lasiren!

The voice he's putting on is like her mother's. Sarah giggles. He goes on.

– I am come. I am tell there is a girl who need my help. A plenty clever girl who know all about the sea. Are you she?

Sarah flings herself off her bed and over to the wall, tries to peep through it.

Through a tiny gap she can see him. He's wearing a green and white African print skirt over his shorts, the zip done up halfway. She recognizes it as her mother's immediately, and claps her hand over her mouth. He must have got it out of the laundry basket! And he has a long-toothed mother of pearl comb poking up from his tightly curled hair. Also her mother's. Tears come to her eyes, half of fear, half of laughter.

– Where did you get those? Richard, Mummy will be so cross! Richard . . .

But he is beckoning her out of the hut to join him. She creeps across the room, holding her breath and staring hard at the dividing wall beyond which her parents sleep, willing them not to wake. She hears the click her mother makes in the back of her nose when she sleeps. She must be extra careful, because if she is caught now, it will be Richard who gets into the most trouble.

Outside, it's oddly quiet. She stands for a moment in her cotton nightdress, then realizes there are no crickets the way there are in Aba Town, with their continuous racket, like a badly tuned radio. There is just the noise of the sea, like the tearing of soft cloth. Richard, with big eyes and his finger to his lips, begins tiptoeing down the sand towards the water with great exaggerated movements. He looks so funny in her mother's skirt! She treads softly after him, trying not to giggle and trying not to notice that the hem of the skirt is dragging in the sand.

Dry sand gives way to damp and now the sea is before them, huge and wrinkled, black and shiny in the moonlight like wet tar. Sarah feels a moment of fear. Is she really going to walk into that?

– Where have the waves gone, Richard?

She speaks in her normal voice, but Richard puts his finger to her lips.

– Sshh! Speak in you small voice only. Or you mamafadder hear.

He crouches down in front of her. The zip strains. She hopes it won't break.

He goes on. – Richard not here tonight, miss. But he tell me you frighten of me and my ocean?

She wants to giggle, but he is looking at her rather seriously. She swallows. Suddenly it seems awful to admit direct to a person's face that she is frightened of them.

– I'm sorry, I don't mean to be frightened. I know it's silly of me and high time I grew out if it.

Richard takes her hand. Behind him the black sea ravels and unravels.

– Is not need for sorry! No need for child so small be sorry!

His Lasiren voice has slipped. She looks at him, surprised. But he coughs and adjusts his comb, and Lasiren comes back, with her high, piping voice. He reaches behind him and produces the shell.

– You friend Richard show me this shell. It plenty big shell! Him tell me you find this shell? I not believe!

Sarah nods seriously. – I did! I did find it! Over there!

She points to the monkey trees, silent away to their right. She wonders where the monkeys are, imagines them hanging asleep in big loops from the branches.

Lasiren whistles admiringly.

– This the biggest shell ever found on this beach. Ever found in the whole of Nigeria.

Sarah beams. Lasiren goes on.

– And what it mean, the one that find it lose all fear of the water!

Sarah frowns. How can her fear be gone, just like that? Lasiren's eyes widen.

– So big this shell, the one that find it not just lose she fear but gain she power to love the water! The water be like she home!

Sarah starts. Home? Is Lasiren going to kidnap her and take her down to a fairy palace at the bottom of the sea? Don't be silly, she tells herself. It's Richard! But even though she knows it's Richard, Lasiren is somehow there too.

– Oh, I'm not sure about that! I don't know if I could actually ever *like* it!

But Lasiren shakes her head firmly. The mother of pearl comb glints in the moonlight.

– Then, Miss Sarah, I believe you were not the girl who found the shell.

Sarah is outraged. – I did, I did! You know I did, Richard!

But Lasiren looks stern.

– I sorry. My business here is finish. I must go. I must go to find the one true girl. The girl who find such beautiful shell.

The injustice burns Sarah. – But I am the one true girl, Lasiren, I am!

But Lasiren just stands. Then she gasps as if she has had a good idea.

– We make test! Is simple. If Miss Sarah is true, then she can step in the water, no problem. If she frighten, we know she is not the one true girl.

– But . . .

– Miss Sarah, you got no choice.

She gets up from Sarah's side, and picks up a stick. On the wet sand, she draws a new moon shape. On top, she draws a mast and a sail, a little pennant. Sarah laughs.

– It's a boat. A sailing boat!

Lasiren smiles and nods towards the sea. – Now we go.

– Just putting my feet in?

– Just, yes.

Lasiren beckons Sarah over. She takes the tails of the nightdress and knots them between Sarah's knees, then she takes the tails of her own skirt and does the same. She holds out her hand to Sarah and the two of them walk down to the edge of the water. They stand, and the water races up silently towards Sarah's toes and covers them. The water is warm; there is no shock. There is only a soft, giving feeling beneath her heels. She gasps, afraid of being sucked down. But Lasiren holds tight to her hand. There's a tickling feeling at her heels, as the water runs quickly back to the sea. When the next surge comes, she is ready for it. At the next, she goes a few steps deeper until the sea tickles the back of her calves.

Her fear seems suddenly like a flat thing, like one side of a coin that can be tossed to show its other side. She walks deeper and deeper, the fabric of her nightdress flopping heavily against her legs as the waves ebb. There is still a glimmer of fear, a shiny edge. It's strange going into the black. You can't see what else might be in there with you. But she lets go of Lasiren's hand and runs a few steps deeper into the sea. It feels like great weights on her legs, blankets wrapped around, pulling her back.

Lasiren is startled. She hisses in Richard's voice.

– Hey, child. You come back now. You no fall!

Sarah stands still, panting, feeling the warm water swelling and falling around her waist.

– Lasiren! Look at me! Shall I go under?

Now Lasiren sounds really alarmed. – Child, no! No get you hair wet!

But it's too late. Sarah closes her eyes, takes a deep breath and ducks down into the water. She stays there for a few seconds. It's cool under the water and quiet, in a thick sort of way, though there's a dull roaring too. She bursts back out, laughing. Lasiren is wading towards her.

– Missy Sarah! Missy Sarah! You OK? Ssshh! Whisper, only! Or I am in plenty plenty trouble. We go back now. We go back.

The green and white skirt floats out around Lasiren's waist like water wings.

– Oh, Richard, stay, let's!

But Lasiren is adamant. She takes Sarah's hand and begins pulling her back to the shore, muttering. The comb has disappeared.

– You hair all wet now. You mama skirt, how I dry before morning?

Sarah lets herself be led back. There is a warm feeling inside her, as if she has made a new friend.

At breakfast, Maureen blinks at the sight of her skirt hanging out to dry.

– I didn't need that skirt yet, Richard. You could have left it till you had a few more things. Have you seen my comb anywhere? Those damned monkeys!

Sarah can hardly swallow her cornflakes. She tries to sound casual.

– I think I might go swimming later, Mummy.

Her mother's coffee cup stops on the way to her mouth. – Really, darling? In the sea?

Sarah hears the hope in her mother's voice, and her heart swells. She nods.

Her mother puts her cup down. – And that'll be all right, will it?

Sarah wonders how to explain. She looks over at Richard, by the window. He raises an eyebrow. A giggle bubbles up inside her, and she swallows it down. Her mother looks curiously at her. Sarah gives up on her cornflakes and pushes the bowl away, longing for the moment when her breakfast will be judged to have gone down.

The Therapist
Mandy Sutter

It started at the hairdresser's, where everyone had an opinion. Barry, with his hips and his scissors, said she should let the attic out to actors.

'£50 a week and no trouble. I know actors.'

Delia on reception, whose hair looked like fancy lettuce, said a regular lodger would be better, then you'd know what you were dealing with. Then they got onto the décor. The girl who swept up the hair said, 'Paint it orange and use it for meditation.' Washing off her lady's perm lotion, even Julie the trainee had an opinion.

'My mam's done ours out all sixties. You know, swirly walls, purple curtains.'

Sylvia Ewen had heard about the sixties, but they were different sixties to the ones she'd lived through, married to Derek.

Barry came across, flourishing a comb. 'Julie, stop trying to influence my ladies. What does Mrs Ewen want with psychedelic lamps? No, my love, white's what you want for actors.'

In front of the big mirror, her voice quavered. 'I shan't be letting it, and there's an end of it. Derek would turn in his grave.'

She saw them exchange glances. But when she got home, smelling of hairspray, she went straight up there. She opened the door carefully. A year on, and she still felt she was intruding. Nicotine-stained walls, tea-stained carpet. Derek had been a forty a day man. He'd had a kettle and tea bags. And he'd not wanted her in to hoover, up there. He'd filled it with all sorts while he was alive, and laid out his model railway in the middle. Now it was all gone, and there were odd dents in the carpet, which no amount of hoovering or scrubbing would shift. He'd spent hours up there, smoking and talking to himself.

She tiptoed over to the dormer and gazed down at the outside world. You could see the city in the distance, like a model city, smaller and more manageable-looking than in real life. And you could see into the neighbours' gardens. She could see a few that needed doing. But most of all you could see sky: great pinky-blue swathes of it. She turned back into the room. Some of the things she'd found! Magazines. Videos. She glanced at the open wardrobe. A brown suit on a hanger. Something of his, to remember him by. Her sister, who'd had a family and knew how to cope, had told her it would be a good idea. Mrs Ewen had gone along with it, numbly. His blue tie – he'd worn his black one in the coffin – hung loosely around the thin neck of the coathanger.

She clasped her hands nervously together. 'It's the money, love,' she said to the suit. 'I could do with it.'

She chose wheat for the walls, white for the ceiling and a beige and brown fleck for the carpet that wouldn't show stains. She got a man out of the paper to do it. As soon as it was finished, she heaved out her cast-iron Olivetti and typed ROOM TO LET on a postcard and put it in the newsagent's window.

*

Mr Thorpe told her right away that he only wanted the room for one day a week. He was a therapist. What kind of therapist she didn't know and didn't ask.

'Will you be giving them, you know, treatment?' she asked.

He was a nothing of a man, thin with a ginger beard and round gold glasses. Not like Derek, who had been a pork butcher right up until the last few weeks of his illness. She hoped he could deal with the difficult cases.

'Of a verbal nature only,' he said cheerily.

'Your patients,' she said. 'What style are they, exactly?'

'Not patients, Mrs Ewen, clients. Clients. People like you and me.'

She doubted it, but straightened the cloth on the hall table and said nothing. She thought of the money. He would occupy the room on Tuesdays between the hours of ten and five. This left six other days when she could let it to someone else.

'Now Mrs E, one more thing,' he said. 'While I'm in occupancy, no hovering in the hall with the Mr Sheen.'

'No, Mr Thorpe.' She had nearly called him 'sir'. It must be the glasses.

'Confidentiality is *vital* to my clients. And if you *should* recognize anybody . . .'

'I'm sure nobody *I* know . . .' she said, indignant.

That first Tuesday morning, she didn't know what to do with herself. She hoovered the room at seven thirty, then again at nine. She drank seven cups of tea. At five to ten, she decided on the front room and, armed with her knitting, turned on the gas fire. She hadn't sat in this room for years, though she tried to keep it nice. The fire gave off a scorching smell. The cuckoo clock had dust on it; she tutted. She had let things go. But it was too late to change rooms now. The first patient would be here any moment.

She wasn't calm enough to sit, so she lurked, stooping behind a vase of white dahlias, her eyes burning a hole in the front path. She'd hated dahlias while Derek was alive. But she'd got into the habit of them and it was too late to change now.

At precisely ten o'clock, a young man with a face like something from *Pet Rescue* pushed open the garden gate. Now she came to think of it, Mr Thorpe had something of the same look, around the eyes. As if they'd seen too much. It must be a certain type. The doorbell rang and she waited for Mr Thorpe to come down, her heart pounding. It was going to put a strain on her, not answering her own front door when it rang. She hoped it wasn't going to finish her off.

She heard low tones in the hall, then the pair of them clomped up the stairs and everything went quiet. Silent even. For forty-five minutes, there was no sound in the house except the soft clip of her own knitting needles. Then, just before the end, there was a cough and – she could have sworn it – laughter. And not a mad cackle, either. Laughter. What did they think this was, Butlins? She regarded the man frostily through her net curtains as he made his way down the path.

The woman who came up the path next was wearing a short tartan skirt and fur-trimmed ankle boots. Too pretty to be having therapy, surely. Mrs Ewen's knitting needles gathered speed. An hour later, the younger Mr Aziz from Dibbs the Chemist came into the garden. Her hand flew to her handbag, beside her on the settee. Was he coming to talk to her about her prescription? Perhaps she'd been on the pills too long; there'd been a programme on telly about how it made people go paranormal. But she'd had to have them, living with Derek. And then, living without him. But then Mr Thorpe was down the stairs and at the door and she realized.

'Well, I never,' she said to her handbag. She knew about Mr Aziz's wife – the whole street did – but she never imagined things had got that bad. 'Well, I never,' she said again. She was almost enjoying herself.

At three o'clock it was a girl, dressed in the grey and navy of the local grammar school. Thin. Mrs Ewen clicked her tongue. An eating disorder of some kind, no doubt. In her day, when there wasn't enough to go round, you wouldn't have got away with it. And yet, she did look pitiful. Out of her element somehow, like a too-big bird. All Mr Thorpe's patients seemed so young. It was sad they had no friends to talk to. That was what they had done in *her* day.

But the last visitor wasn't young. She was a small round woman of about Mrs Ewen's own age. She scuttled up the path, knuckles white from clutching her battered brown handbag tight to her stomach. Her grey hair lay flattened on her head. Mrs Ewen patted her own coiffure, blue-white and stiffened with hairspray, and glanced at the mirror above the fire for reassurance. She waited for the doorbell to ring. But it didn't. She listened and listened, straining her hearing until it felt as if someone was playing the drums inside her head. Still the bell didn't ring. The woman stood unannounced on the doorstep for a good five minutes. Mrs Ewen could hardly bear it. At last, the bell rang and Mr Thorpe came clattering down the stairs. Mrs Ewen pressed her ear to the door.

'I didn't like to disturb you before four,' she heard the poor woman say.

'Yes indeed,' said Mr Thorpe, 'I'm afraid there is no waiting room here.'

'The bus gets me here at a quarter to, you see. I'd have been late if I'd waited till the twenty-five to . . .' Their voices tailed away up the stairs.

Mrs Ewen found it difficult to concentrate on her knitting pattern while the woman was upstairs. What was a pensioner doing, having therapy? She knew enough about Mr Thorpe's fee scale and enough about pensions to know that the one wouldn't go very far towards the other. It seemed hours later when the woman came downstairs, struggled with the front door and was released back onto the garden path. Mrs Ewen watched her go. There was a soft tap at the front-room door.

'Not disturbing you, Mrs E, I hope . . . my dear, is something wrong?'

She turned. The therapist looked kind, like Jesus. She wanted to throw herself onto his feet and weep. She sat down.

'No, Mr Thorpe. I just came over a bit . . .'

He took a step towards her, but she gripped her knitting tightly to her chest.

'I trust the room was how you wanted it,' she said, stiffly.

'Yes, Mrs E.' He sighed. 'The room was admirable.'

When Mr Thorpe had gone, and she had drunk three cups of tea, she found that she'd made a mistake in her knitting and would have to unpick it all the way back to the armholes. Not, she thought – with an unfamiliar surge of bitterness – that her niece was ever likely to appreciate the work that was going into this cardigan. She'd never worn the last one, not even at Christmas.

The nights drew in. Every Tuesday, the same patients came and went. She got used to them. She didn't bother to let the room out on other days. She noticed and approved the pretty woman's new winter coat. She came to expect the scruffy man's loud laughter at the end of his sessions. She began to feel a bit freer in the house while patients were upstairs. She popped to and fro from the kitchen to the back room. Instead of darting up to the lavatory and straight back down again, she got on with things upstairs if she needed to, doing the odd bit in the bedrooms and on the upstairs landing. Though if she heard any major noise from the attic room, she would scuttle back down into the front room and close the door smartly behind her. And she was always in there on the hour. She liked to know who was in the house.

But she didn't get used to the small round woman, who went on arriving five minutes early and standing on the doorstep until the cuckoo clock struck four. If only she would go and look at the shops in the parade for five minutes instead. When she was standing outside waiting like that, all humble, Mrs Ewen didn't feel right with herself.

While the woman was upstairs, she would sit and knit feverishly. When she heard distant sounds that might have been crying, her knitting needles would freeze and sometimes she would drop a stitch. Once, she thought she heard a scream and ran, heart pounding, halfway up the stairs with a box of tissues. And when she came back downstairs, she left the door to the front room ajar, just in case the woman wanted to come in and talk, another woman being perhaps better, in some cases, than a man, but the woman left with her head down, the way a man might leave a brothel. Mrs Ewen decided to have a word when Mr Thorpe came to pay his rent.

'Ah,' he said.

His lack of apology or explanation made her say more than she'd intended. She heard herself babble on about how she didn't mean to overhear things, really she didn't, but how sometimes she couldn't help it, there being no point in having the radio on, not nowadays, not on a Tuesday, not since Jimmy Young left. And how the poor unhappy woman's sobs had cut right through her like a knife through butter. The therapist still didn't say anything, just looked at her gravely and nodded. It made her feel awful.

Exposed. And then she felt cross with him, for letting her go on like that.

On the last Tuesday afternoon before Christmas, it started to snow. The small round woman arrived at the front door a whole quarter of an hour early, while the anorexic school-girl was still upstairs with Mr Thorpe. Mrs Ewen strode to and fro behind her nets. Which was worse, to break Mr Thorpe's rule about no contact, or to allow one patient to run into another?

A sound upstairs galvanized her and she dashed into the hall. Her hands shook on the Yale. The woman, who had been standing with her back to the door, jumped.

Mrs Ewen felt breathless. 'Would you like to come in for a bit of a sit down?' she asked.

Close-up, the woman looked even older than Mrs Ewen had supposed, with jowly cheeks like an old dog, and watery blue eyes.

'That's kind of you,' she said. She sounded posher than Mrs Ewen had supposed, too. 'But I'm fine here. To tell you the truth I like being in the air.'

Mrs Ewen could feel the air getting into the house, cold and solid. But now she had opened the door, she didn't like to shut it again. She stepped out and pulled the door half shut behind her. The woman made room for her on the step and they stood next to each other, facing out. The air was thick and whirling. She could feel it getting into her lungs. Flakes of snow dissolved into the pink fluff on her slippers.

'Are you one of Mr Thorpe's clients, too?' the woman asked gently.

'What, me? Goodness, no. I *live* here!'

Mrs Ewen rearranged herself on the step. 'Not,' she added, 'that there's owt wrong with it.'

There was another silence.

'Aren't you cold in just your cardi?' said the woman. 'I'm all right out here, I really am. If you want to go back inside . . .'

Mrs Ewen frowned. 'Do you . . . just sit and talk to him, up there?'

'Why, I suppose so, yes. I suppose that's about it.'

'But . . . don't it feel wrong, telling a man – a stranger – all them things, private things?'

'Well, yes, it did at first. But I got used to it.'

'I'm not sure it's summat I'd want to get used to.'

The woman turned suddenly and touched Mrs Ewen lightly on the shoulder. Her eyes danced.

'Anyway,' she said, 'it's not for ever, you know. It's my last session today.'

'You what?' Mrs Ewen's insides swarmed unpleasantly. 'You mean that's it, all over with?'

The door opened behind them and the anorexic girl burst out onto the step.

'Snow,' she said, looking from one to the other, 'cool!' Then she was off, skidding this way and that on the path.

'I'd better be getting up there,' said the woman. She hesitated. 'Is everything all right?'

But Mrs Ewen just stood there, staring up at the teeming sky, unable to speak.

Sidura Ludwig

SIDURA LUDWIG is a Canadian writer who lived in Birmingham from 2001 to 2004. Her short fiction has appeared in UK magazines and anthologies, and has won the Canadian Author and Bookman First Prize for Most Promising Writer. Sidura now lives in Winnipeg, where she is completing her first novel, *Holding My Breath*.

Ten Ways to Better Customer Relations

Sidura Ludwig

After opening her card shop and then observing other small businesses in Winnipeg, Cathy decided that someone needed to write an idiot's guide to customer relations. A top ten list. Every night, before she went to sleep, Cathy thought about her customers that day and how she'd handled them. If she did something particularly right, like guess the scent of hand cream they'd like by their perfume, Cathy wrote it down in her journal. After a while, the list looked something like this:

Cathy's Top Ten Guide to Better Customer Relations

1. Be attentive – notice your customer's taste by looking at their clothes, jewellery, glasses, etc. You can know what they'd like before they ask for your help.

2. Play soft music, but not always classical. Keep a CD collection of local folk artists. People feel special when they hear local music.

3. Always smile.

And so on.

She planned, when she completed this guide, to type it up and paste it behind the counter so that the girls could internalize it. Like a policy. They were pretty good, her girls. Only once did she catch Sarah Jane arguing with a man about his change. She had forgotten to give him his five-dollar bill with his forty-six cents. Just plain forgot. The man finally had to go through his receipt in front of her and when she realized what she had done she placed the bill on the counter and then walked to the back of the store where she cried out of humiliation. Cathy let her be for twenty minutes and then she was fine.

That same night, Cathy started another list called *Ten Ways to Better Staff Relations*:

1. *Give them their space.*

2. *Let them make mistakes.*

3. *Thank them when they make extra effort – not all the time otherwise it starts to sound false.*

Etcetera.

Cathy's girls came to her from the university. They worked for her around their class schedules, and when the store wasn't busy, they exchanged tips on mean-spirited professors, post-colonial Canadian storytelling, and which second-hand clothing shops had the best deals. Cathy had twelve employees altogether, all part-time, including seven students, one friend whose children had either married or moved away, and four young dancers from the studio across the street. She structured her employee schedule carefully, so that the dancers were never in the store on their own (this had nothing to do with trust, but was more to do with safety. The dancers were no more than eighteen years old and all less than a hundred pounds), and either she or her friend were in the store at all times. Also, she found products in her line of business sold better when a more mature woman was present and appeared to be in charge.

As well as cards, Cathy carried handmade jewellery, spiritual relaxation CDs, journals and scented candles. She also sold a selection of body products made locally by a woman on a farm outside of Selkirk. Customers who came regularly remarked that they could always be sure to find something different at Cathy's. Some of them found they couldn't buy something for someone else without making a purchase for themselves as well. Cathy never forced products on people – and she made sure her staff knew not to as well. What she was particularly talented at was talking to her customers, finding out their stories and then casually mentioning a new item in which they might be interested – lavender eye pillows for women who'd been working late at the office, aromatherapy diffusers for students with head colds, a hand-woven throw to cover a sagging futon. People left Cathy's feeling like they had been given a gift. Often, they forgot they had spent any money at all.

When she started out, Cathy called her business Cathy's Cards, because she used to design her own with pressed flowers, dried leaves and thin, Japanese paper. When she bought the storefront in Osborne Village, she dropped 'Cards' and just called it Cathy's. As if people were coming over to visit.

It's not that she was lonely – please, she wouldn't want you to think that. Cathy had a daughter, Abby, who lived with her and studied law at the University of Manitoba (she also took three shifts in the store during the week). When they shared shifts at the store, people mistook them for sisters. (Cathy, who was of Ukrainian heritage, had plump skin and a short, blond bob. She'd always looked younger than she was.) She had elderly parents in the Wellesley Retirement Centre, whom she visited on Wednesday evenings and Sunday mornings. She had her closest girl-friend, Doreen, who agreed all too eagerly to come work in her store when she told her she was expanding out of her basement craft workshop ('Whatever you need,' Doreen told her. 'After all this time, it's so good to see you moving on.' And to her husband who questioned why she would want to go work in retail, now: 'I'll do anything to help Cathy get back into the real world.'). Both women were short, round, and wore turtleneck knit sweaters with hand-crafted brooches and woven silk scarves. Cathy had the university girls who cried on her shoulder when their boy-friends were playing up, and she had her dancer girls who made friendship bracelets and beaded earrings, and came running to show her first when they had their braces off.

When Cathy first opened the store, it was like she had given birth to an enormous family that kept expanding whenever someone new came in. After years of shutting herself away to care for her sick husband; of lying awake night after night once he was gone, shaking in their empty bed; and then years later of staying in to make sure that Abby had everything she needed, even if she didn't have a father – Cathy felt she wasn't in a position to turn anyone away who needed looking after. Soon after the store opened, and it became obvious that people were drawn to it not just for the pretty things, but because talking to Cathy was like cheap therapy, Doreen turned to her and said, 'Dollface, you were meant to be a matriarch of a huge clan.'

Cathy blushed a bit, but on her way to the back of the store, she smiled, thinking, *Maybe I am. Maybe this is it.*

Many shop owners in Winnipeg hate Christmas. The late-night inventory and then sub-zero temperatures to the car in darkened parking lots; the cold, frantic customers, burst-ing into stores as if the wind outside had pushed them in against their will; the children with woollen mittens sticky from peppermint candy canes, and the mess they left on glass shelving units. If it weren't for the profits, many would close up over December and move to Palm Springs. Except for Cathy. She played CBC2 on the radio with Jurgen Goth, and filled the store with a cappella groups and harpsichord versions of 'God Rest Ye Merry Gentlemen'. She offered customers free hot cinnamon coffee, and shortbread for the children. She decorated her store in tinsel and stained-glass stars and sold hand-carved wooden tree ornaments. One evening she stayed late with Abby to erect the Christmas tree, only to find that the dancers from across the street were waiting to sing her carols and to give her a cup of hot chocolate.

They all stayed around to help decorate the tree, and in all of the commotion of sparkling streamers, tissue snowflakes and giggling, Cathy didn't notice the tall man bundled in a tweed coat and a thick, brown knit scarf making his way out of the falling snow and into the doorway that should have been locked. He stamped his feet lightly on the mat, announcing his presence, but no one was listening, and then made his way to the side of the store where the body lotions were.

Abby saw him first. 'Mum,' she said, in a whisper. 'Should he be in here?'

Cathy looked up and saw him picking the lotions up and putting them back in a fluid motion, as if the bottles might burst if he held them for too long.

Cathy hung her wooden angel and waded through the girls around the tree to get to the other end of the store.

'Excuse me,' she said to the man, who, startled, backed away from the shelving unit and began to look around, realizing that the lights were off and that he was the only customer in the store. The first thing Cathy noticed was that she couldn't tell the colour of his eyes; they were green and blue with specks of brown. His nose was slightly crooked near the ridge, and his skin was dry, flaking where he had shaved that morning.

'We're not actually open,' Cathy said. The man had pale lips and silver hair, shot with black escaping from his cap. 'But is there anything I can help you with?'

He spoke softly. 'Do you have any rose-water hand cream?' he asked, and then, 'I'm so sorry to bother you. I assumed you were open. I can come back . . .'

Cathy was already looking through the bottles on the shelf. 'I know we have some on order, but I don't see any here. It will probably be in the shipment coming tomorrow. Would you like some vanilla hand cream instead?'

'No,' the man said, tightening his scarf. 'I'll have to come back. Really sorry to bother you. And the girls. I didn't mean to get in the way of the party.'

'You didn't,' Cathy said, walking with him to the door. She only came up to his shoulder. His coat smelled like wet wool and cedar. 'Come back tomorrow. I'll have some then.'

He tipped his hat as he walked away.

The next day when the shipment arrived, Cathy put a bottle of the hand cream behind the counter. Rule number six from her Better Customer Relations list was to always remember requests. She didn't know the man's name, so she wrote on a sticky note, 'Tall man, soft voice, tweed cap', and stuck it on the bottle. He came into the store near the end of the day, and Cathy put the bottle onto the front counter as he came through the door. She put the sticky note in her pocket.

'Thank you,' he said gently, reaching for his wallet. 'My wife will be so pleased.'

'Is this a Christmas gift?' Cathy asked. 'Do you want me to wrap it for you?'

'No, it's not,' he said. 'It's just something she's been asking for a lot lately. It's always been her favourite. I'll take it in the bag. That will be fine.'

'Your wife is very lucky to have a husband who buys her presents for no reason,' Cathy said. She put the bottle into a paper bag with a straw handle, and tied it up with ribbon to look festive.

The man's cheeks flushed a bit pink, back to his earlobes. It may have been the cold, but still Cathy looked away so as not to embarrass him further. 'Yes, well,' he tried and then, because he didn't really have anything to add, he let out a long sigh, like the weight of his body sinking into a seat.

'Many thanks for this. I'll see you again.'

'You're welcome,' Cathy said. 'Merry Christmas.'

She did see him again. Monday the following week, he came into the store at lunchtime and looked at the gift cards. Cathy was at the back of the store and she watched him from her seat at the computer. He would never know that she could look at him from there, staring, camouflaged by the boxes, invoices and the busyness she was meant to be involved with. He looked at the birthday cards with six-line poems. He picked up a purple one with an embossed image of a lily, read it through, and then put it back. Cathy thought to show him her collection of handmade cards, but that would mean getting up and losing her privileged position. He stood stooped with his head tilted to one side, reading each card in the row. When he had read them all, he left.

Sometimes, in the evening, Cathy missed her husband's hand finding her shoulder, rubbing her neck without her asking. It had been a long time since she had felt it, and she was always surprised how intense the longing could be. That evening, sitting on her couch, wrapped in a quilted throw, Cathy had a flash of the Tweed Man's hand, palm dry, fingers gently manipulating her neck muscles. The image came and left her so suddenly, she didn't know whether to feel lonely or giddy.

Over the busy Christmas period it was difficult for Cathy to spend quality time with her customers. She particularly liked to talk to people visiting the city, especially those from out East, who, despite the cold, always remarked how friendly Winnipeg was. She felt it her duty, like an ambassador, to prove their theory, and she would ask them all kinds of questions about their travels, while suggesting little-known tourist spots to visit. However, in December, the best she could hope for was to smile at the shoppers and maybe dig up an old memory to impress them with.

'How did your mother like those earrings?'

'Have you had a chance to try the bath balms yet?'

'Is your wife enjoying the rose-water cream?'

'Yes,' he answered, while purchasing some refrigerator magnets, a collection of six pressed Manitoba flowers. 'She puts it on the morning and then again in the evening.' He let go of a quick laugh. 'Sometimes it's like sleeping in a flower bed.'

'At least you have sweet dreams,' she said to him. One of her lessons in customer relations was to be interested in what they are telling you, but not too nosy. This was becoming difficult with the man in the tweed coat. She found herself noticing the smell of his spicy aftershave and wondering whether he was the type of man to shower in the morning, the evening, or even both? She would have listened to him tell her how he made his coffee in the morning, if he had wanted. She imagined his wife, graceful but not young, with creamy, soft skin. Cathy imagined that he watched his rose-scented wife sleeping beside him, grateful that she had slept in that same spot for the last forty years or so. Did he lie awake, in love with this scent? Did she get to claim any part, for having sold it to him?

He was signing his credit card receipt when Cathy said all of a sudden, 'I'm thinking of adding a book section to the shop. Gifty things – like cookbooks and coffee table books. And then maybe an area for local writers. What do you think?'

'Oh,' he said, taking a step back, putting his wallet away inside his jacket. She thought of her guide and decided to add another point to it that evening: *Make your customers feel important.*

'Oh, well. I think that's a great idea. I'm sure you'd make it work. Yes, well done.'

And with that he straightened his cap and left.

Doreen whistled from behind the counter. Something like 'Santa Claus Is Coming to Town', but Cathy wasn't sure.

It was only when she was tidying up the store, and Doreen had already gone home, that Cathy found the credit card. David E. Wiffen. She wondered what the E stood for. All this time she hadn't known his name and yet she had never imagined he would have a middle name as well. Edward? Ethan? Ezra? Was it fair to be given only partial information? And she didn't want to wait until she saw him next to find out. There was only one Wiffen, D. in the phone book, on Waterloo Street, number 847. When she dialled the number, there was no answer; so Cathy placed the card in her pocket, locked up the store and decided to stop off there on her way home.

David E. Wiffen's house was a bungalow set back from the road by a long lawn. The living-room window faced the front street and the curtains were drawn back, even though it was evening. Some Christmas lights flickered on and off around the window, red and blue winks, shaped like icicles.

It had been a windy day, and dry snow had blown onto the porch and walkway, making tiny, frozen waves over the sidewalk which otherwise had been recently cleared. It looked like David used a snow-clearing service and Cathy thought, Good. He's too old to be shovelling heavy snow himself.

The lights were on inside the house and when she rang the doorbell she heard shuffling and muffled voices.

'I'll be right there,' he called. There were sounds from the kitchen: a setting down of pans and dishes; something small, like cutlery, falling to the floor.

David opened the door halfway and stuck his head around. A woman from inside called, 'Who is it? Who's there?'

'Don't worry,' he called back. 'I've got it.'

Then he turned to Cathy. 'Oh, hello. Did I forget something?'

'Yes.' She reached inside her pocket for the card, which felt even stiffer from the cold. 'Your credit card. I found it after you left. There was only on D. Wiffen in the phone book.'

'Yoowhoo,' called the woman. 'Who's there? Who's talking?'

'Don't worry, Edith. I'm right here by the door,' he answered. Cathy could hear Edith in the kitchen, mumbling *oh dear, oh dear* over and over again to herself.

'My wife gets anxious when she can't see me,' he said to Cathy, his voice low, as if apologizing. 'She gets confused very easily. Thank you for coming by. That was very kind of you. I hope it wasn't out of your way.'

'No,' Cathy said. But she felt very out of her way. Very much on a porch where she should never have stood. 'You're on my way home.'

David closed the door and Cathy watched her breath hanging in front of her, frozen.

*

After that, Cathy stopped day-dreaming. She stopped pretending that David's graceful wife was herself. She had used to wonder what his lips, a bit chapped and cool from the icy wind, would feel like against her forehead at the end of the day. She stopped all of that, and concentrated on dusting her shop, on arranging the candles and picture frames so that they looked fresh. She bought an advent calendar and all her girls told her to stop feeding them so much chocolate because they were getting too fat. She added more points to her list, such as: *Throw scented beads into gift bags with the tissue paper* and *Develop promotions customers can participate in, like* My Favourite Thing about Winnipeg *and* Top Ten Christmas Songs.

She stayed up late in her workshop and made earrings for each of her employees, choosing beads to match their eye colour and bending the gold wire with tweezers into curls and boxes. When she held the jewellery in front of her, they span like mini-mobiles, the beads catching the lamplight and twinkling.

At the store, Doreen came by one early morning when she wasn't scheduled to.

'I just need a little something,' she said. 'You don't mind that I've come by? To do my Christmas shopping? You know I'd rather give you the business.'

'You look tired,' she continued. 'You're working too hard again, aren't you?'

'Yes,' said a man's voice. 'She is. Not that she would admit it.'

David had come up behind Doreen, carrying two Styrofoam cups. The lids were open a bit and steam rose quickly, attracted to the crisp morning air.

'Hmm,' Doreen said, turning away. She whistled again. This time she whistled 'Mr. Sandman' very obviously.

David set the cups down on the counter and took off his hat, as if staying for the morning. Cathy hadn't had a chance to vacuum and the carpet was gritty from wet boots and salt.

'One is for you,' he said, while she stood, watching. Doreen stayed by the candles, but not too far away. 'Please have some.'

'You didn't have to,' Cathy said. She had spent so much energy forgetting him that his face peering down at her caught her breath and she struggled for a moment to find it again. She had learned, after that night when she stood on his porch, that there is a limit to how much one should know about one's customers. That's what she wrote in her journal. Rule number 11: *Know when to stop*. She wanted to serve all of her patrons with respect, and none with pity.

Still, she lifted the cup to her lips.

'This is what I should have done when you came by,' David explained. 'The proper thing would have been to ask you in for a hot drink.'

'No, not at all. I didn't want to disturb you.'

'I would have dropped in sooner, but Edith hasn't been well these last couple of weeks, and I've had to rush home to relieve the careworker.'

This was knowing too much. Now they were talking like friends. Now she was invited into his life because she'd returned his credit card. And he expected her to accept the invitation because he'd brought her coffee.

'It's been very busy here because of the holiday,' she answered.

He sipped his coffee and they were both silent, surveying the store, realizing who they were to each other – no one yet. Just a customer and a sales woman. But now there was this potential.

'Well,' he said. Doreen was making her way to the counter with a bouquet of scented candles. 'I should get to the office. Traffic's a bit slow. They haven't cleared all the streets yet.'

'This was very nice,' she said. Now Doreen was standing behind him, peering over his shoulder, eyebrows raised. 'I really needed this coffee this morning. Thank you for thinking of me.'

He put his hat on and stood up straight, stretching his shoulders back without raising his arms. He laughed, nervously.

'And I really needed my credit card the other night. So the favour is returned.'

He said 'Excuse me' to Doreen and left the store.

She couldn't stop the fantasies after that. She didn't even try. At night she abandoned her lists and imagined lying in bed with David, his knees curled and bent against the back of hers as they slept, his breath warm on her shoulder. She imagined his arms around her waist, his hands rubbing her stomach, her breasts, and then she kissing his fingers. Sometimes the shadow of his wife got in the way and Cathy felt a bit like a murderer making her disappear. Then she lay there, in bed, not sleeping, steeped instead in guilt, as though she had committed a crime with no one to apologize to.

The day before Christmas Eve, Cathy kept the store open until ten p.m., although people had stopped coming in by nine thirty. She let Sarah Jane go early because she could close up on her own and she wanted to do some tidying anyway. She was already planning her post-Christmas inventory and considering ordering pizza for her staff who would be staying late. Or maybe she would make it herself with the bread machine she knew she was getting from Abby for Christmas. What a nice way to break it in.

Cathy hadn't yet locked the door and had just begun shutting off the lights when the bell went, sounding much louder in the dark. She jumped and David, seeing her frightened, backed away from the doorway.

'I'm sorry,' he said. 'I hoped you were still open. I can come back tomorrow . . .'

Cathy caught her breath, her heart still pounding. 'It's cold out,' she managed. 'Come in and close the door.'

David stood by the door and looked around the store as though he had forgotten why he'd come. There was only one light on, like a spotlight, by the till. He stayed near the light, as though the rest of the store was off limits, until Cathy said, 'I haven't counted out yet, if you need anything.'

He cleared his throat. 'Yes,' he said, now remembering. 'Yes. I promised I would bring home some more of that cream. Edith likes it quite a lot, you know. When she was a girl, her grandfather grew rose bushes. So, I think the smell brings her good memories.'

He found the bottle in the dark and Cathy met him at the cash register. As she typed in the purchase, he spoke with the weighted, soft tone of intimacy.

'Have you ever lost someone you love?'

'Yes,' she replied, remaining professional to wrap the bottle in tissue paper and place it in the paper bag, adding the scented beads, tying everything with a ribbon.

'How did you move on?'

She handed him his purchase and his change.

'I had my daughter to look after. She needed a loving mother and so I spent my time loving her.'

He folded the top of the bag so it was closed more tightly. He stood staring at the counter, searching for his words.

'Edith's been offered a place in a home,' he said. 'It's not far, but if we're going to take it, we have to take it now because there are plenty of people who could have the spot.'

He stood before her, depleted and completely open.

'I don't know why I am telling you this. It's just very hard at home, alone. And I don't think I can do it any more.'

He didn't look up when he spoke. Cathy considered that he wasn't really speaking to her at all. She put her hand on his arm and said, 'You do take very good care of her.'

He put his hand on top of hers and rubbed it lightly. His palms were rough with age and winter. The skin around his nails was dry and peeling. He had faint freckles around his knuckles and one cluster looked like a star.

'I miss talking to her. I talk to her a lot but she hasn't the patience to sustain a conversation with me. That's what I miss the most.'

That won't come back, Cathy thought, but didn't say it. He sighed as if to say he knew and squeezed her hand before looking up and letting go.

'Right,' he said. 'It will be a busy weekend.'

She walked him to the door. 'You don't need to buy something to come by,' she said. 'And you don't need to bring me coffee either.'

This made him smile. He reached out his hand to rub her shoulder, but instead ran his thumb along her cheek and jawbone. Cathy didn't move. It was as if she felt the glove with every inch of her face. She smelled the buckskin leather, a bit moist from the snow. His hand was so big that the glove came close to her mouth and she could nearly taste it. His hand rested then at the base of her neck, his palm on her shoulder. She placed her hand on top of his, and after a moment he had to pull away, tightening his scarf, hesitating before heading back into the snow, and the cold.

Interlake Evergreens

Sidura Ludwig

The first time David slept with Cathy he held her all night and listened to her breathe. He didn't sleep. He couldn't. He wasn't used to her blonde hair resting beneath his chin. Or the way she slept with one hand covering her mouth and nose, like she'd fallen asleep in the middle of a yawn. And he wasn't used to her bed; for the last forty years or so his had always been soft, king size and full of blankets because Edith often felt cold at night. But Cathy used only a crisp cotton sheet in the summer (she kept a Hudson Bay blanket in the closet for really cold nights), and she slept in a double bed because anything bigger was too lonely and a single was too depressing

He lay in bed feeling drunk. He had been in the same position all night, on his back and looking up at her ceiling. She had old mouldings that circled the top of her walls like a crown. They were even painted gold. He wondered what it would be like to wake up to this ceiling and beneath this crown every morning. He looked around the room, his eyes adjusted to the dark, and caught sight of the picture of Cathy's daughter, Abby, now a lawyer in Toronto, looking down at him from the wall, smiling in her graduation cape. He felt as if he should get up out of the bed and explain this all to her; wrap a towel around his waist and try telling her frozen face just how painfully and joyfully he had fallen for her mother. And then for the hundredth time that night he wondered what he was doing and how he'd got there. Cathy hadn't moved from where she slept and he felt her breathe against his chest in small, rhythmic puffs. She didn't wear perfume, only baby powder, and that's what David smelled while she slept against him. He lay there wishing that the sun wouldn't come up so that he didn't have to face all of his questions in the daylight.

But the sun did come up. Cathy woke around seven, her face pressed deep into his chest. She looked almost child-like and David wondered if all women did when they were sleeping. Because he remembered thinking the same thing about Edith.

'Good morning,' she mumbled into his skin. He kissed her forehead which was warm, salty and tasted familiar, having rested against him for much of the night.

'Good morning,' David whispered, liking the intimacy of them being alone and wanting that to last longer.

She stretched and he watched her legs shift under the covers. Cathy's legs were short, her thighs plump and round. However, when she pointed her toes her foot arched like a ballerina's. David wondered how long it would take him to get used to sleeping beside someone full. Edith had always been so tiny and precious, he had often been afraid of rolling the wrong way and smothering her in the night.

'Did you sleep all right?' she asked.

'Yes,' he lied, 'Just fine.'

It was a Sunday morning and neither of them had to go into work. Cathy had her friend Doreen minding the store so that they could spend the day together. It was the August long weekend and David planned to take her to the Interlake and Gimli to see some of the Icelandic Festival. She had never been and he hadn't walked along the beach in years. Earlier in the summer, when they'd discussed the weekend, she'd thought it sounded wonderful. But then, Cathy always seemed happy whatever they were doing. That amazed David – that she was happy just to spend time with him.

She sat up in bed and he rubbed her back. Her skin was doughy and it gathered just above her waistline. David loved it, though. Kneading her with his hands, feeling her body warm against his palms. She sighed against his massage and turned over to lie on top of him.

'Why don't we just stay here?' she whispered as David moved his hands all over her, just to believe she was real.

They were on the road by ten, a little bit later if you count the stop they made at Robin's Donuts for coffee. This had always been David's route. When he and Edith used to drive out to Gimli for the day they took Highway 7 because of Robin's Donuts. When they were younger they got donuts as well as coffee – a selection of six so that Edith could have her jam buster and David could have his maple dip. This time, he and Cathy bought coffee and low-fat muffins. The steam from the coffee hung on his upper lip and nose as he raised the paper cup to his mouth. The coffee tasted the same. Why couldn't that have changed? he thought. He gave a quick laugh out loud, which made Cathy turn. She looked like an Icelandic elf – short, straight blonde hair cut like an eight-year-old boy's, round face that pinched her pink cheeks when she smiled. Her dimples came out just below her blue eyes. That's where David had started kissing her the night before. She would never age, he thought, sipping his coffee again. And somewhere, deep inside his stomach, he felt a kernel of envy blooming.

'You all right?' she asked.

'Just fine.'

*

The drive isn't long from Winnipeg to Gimli. An hour at most. David drove along Highway 7 north, and then made a right at Fraserwood. Cathy spent most of the ride staring out the window at the cattle grazing, the odd horse sunning himself.

'Look at that,' she said, more to herself than to David, as they passed a black stallion. Then, 'I always wanted to ride a horse. It looks very majestic. Have you ever been? Horseback riding?'

He shook his head, keeping his eyes on the road. 'Edith and I thought to go once, and then she was too frightened when we stood beside the horses. They can be massive animals. No, we watched the others instead and walked around the farm. Actually, it wasn't too far from here. The farm. I wonder if they still offer riding?'

'Maybe we can go,' Cathy said. 'Not today, but maybe one day.'

'Sure,' he answered. 'Maybe.'

He was grateful for her patience. It was over eighteen months since they first met and she never tired of him speaking about Edith. At first David was hesitant to share his memories with her, figuring she'd prefer them to create their own. But that wasn't what she wanted. She said to him, 'I don't want you to pretend she doesn't exist just because you're with me now. That's not fair to either of us.'

So he stopped pretending. He took her through photo albums, showed her letters and told her stories. Lots of stories. Not so much out of desperation to live the moments again, but more out of a desire to have her live them with him. And then, when she'd heard enough (because he could go on and on), she'd put her hands on top of his and say, 'OK. Let's just be us now.'

The first time she did that David was so shocked by the feel of her silky hands that he actually caught his breath. And then he held her hands firm in his own and leaned over to kiss her. She took him gently, her mouth relaxed, moist. But he felt her sigh, as if she had been holding her breath for a long time and now, finally, she could let it go.

When they got into Gimli, David parked the car on First Avenue, close to the entrance to Loni Beach. It was already hot when they got there – the early August morning breeze had backed away into a heat that descended upon them like a wall. Cathy, ever organized, made sure they were covered in sunscreen and, though David never wore hats, she bought him a baseball cap for the occasion. Winnipeg Goldeyes baseball team – their symbol a fish ready to hit a home run. She wore one too, and they matched. In the summer, Edith used to wear long, loose dresses and, when she was young, her dark hair tied in a scarf at the back of her head. David closed his eyes to stop comparing.

'It's lovely out here,' Cathy said, slipping out of the car. She wore khaki shorts and a white T-shirt with embroidered butterflies. From two blocks away, they could hear squeals and screams mixed with loud popular music from the Icelandic Festival fairground. Normally, Gimli would be stiller – all the noise concentrated down by the beach. With the fair, the town felt like one big carnival, with no place to escape for those no longer interested in cotton candy and mini-donuts.

'Where to first?' she asked, stretching her arms above her head and then relaxing her shoulders and reaching for his hand. David took her hand in his and they walked silently for a while. He wondered if her hand felt different now, if maybe they walked more comfortably together. More like a couple. She seemed as relaxed as she had always been this last year. Cathy had a way of keeping in control when David could feel his world unravelling.

'Let me show you the town first,' he said. 'Then we can go to the beach. Maybe later we'll go to the fair. It's up to you.'

'I'd like to see the water,' she said.

They hadn't talked about the night before. David wasn't sure if this was because it was so natural, or because they were afraid to admit something had changed. David didn't talk to women the way he talked with Cathy. Not even Edith. Edith and David had been a team, but that meant they each had roles – husband, wife, parents, but never friends. His friends were the men with whom he played squash, their friends were couples with whom they went to the symphony. That's not to say he didn't love her. He did. Fiercely. Because they fitted into each other's lives filling the gaps neither knew were there. Walking with Cathy, feeling her fingers slide through his own, he felt his stomach fold into ripples. What gaps would they fill for each other?

'Oh, David,' Cathy said. 'This really is something.'

In all fairness, Gimli is nothing special. The main street downtown has a tea-room, merchant's shop, grocer, ice-cream stand and hotel. There is the pier, which lately the town had commissioned artists to decorate with paintings of local images. Cathy wanted ice cream and then a walk along the pier. David let her take him wherever she wanted.

'David,' she said as they stepped onto the wooden planks by the water. She licked her maple walnut cone. He sipped a chocolate milkshake. 'How often did you come out here with Edith?'

'Once a year,' he answered. He leaned on the cement wall and looked out at the children playing in the lake. One group had a beach ball and when one tried to throw it to the other, it blew in the opposite direction.

Then, very casually, she asked. 'Do you wish you were here with her right now?'

Cathy had a way of asking questions like that about Edith. David thought she worried she was getting in the way of his memories. Or that she was becoming a replacement.

'I wish for both things,' he said, because Cathy deserved his honesty. 'I wish I could be here with Edith as I knew her, and as I was with her. And I wish I could be here with you, as we are now.'

Then he put his arm around her and drew her in so that he could kiss her forehead. Yes, he thought, smelling her hair, the lake wind, feeling his stomach relax and melt with gratitude – he wished he could live two lives.

In the end, they decided that the beach was too busy and Cathy was intrigued by the sounds of the fair at the park. Everything in Gimli is walking distance, and that suited Cathy who liked to walk. They entered the park from the opposite end of the fair, where all the children's climbing equipment is. Of course, there were no children playing on the swings because nothing could top the Ferris Wheel or the Tilt-A-Whirl. There were lots of young evergreens, though. All chest height with bright needles.

Some years back, there had been a tornado in Gimli which had wiped out most of the evergreen trees. Three summers ago, the town planted new trees and David realized that was the last time he and Edith had been in Gimli together. Already, Edith had been feeling wary about leaving familiar surroundings, but David convinced her to go to Gimli for the day. He tried to tell her that she liked being out in the country and by the lake, but she didn't remember.

They happened to get to the town just around the time the mayor was planting the first new tree. People were buying trees and planting them in honour of loved ones, or just because of the memories they had of being in Gimli.

'Where are we?' Edith asked, rubbing her palms toether as if to keep warm. But this was what she did when she was nervous.

'This is Gimli, dear. You've been here with me before. It's just been a while.'

At first she didn't want to leave the car. She said she could view the town just fine through the window. But finally David told her he needed to get out to stretch his legs and wouldn't she please join him?

'David,' she said. 'You are so persistent.'

He got her out and as soon as she felt the sun on her face, she started to smile. They walked arm-in-arm to the park and he pointed out the tree planting and told her why people were doing it.

'Would you like to buy a tree?' he asked her.

'Yes, I think that would be appropriate.'

A young girl sold them a baby evergreen and explained how to plant it and which areas of the park were designated for trees. Edith, all at once, became very enthusiastic. She spotted a corner of the park where the tree would grow to shade a sandbox.

'This is just lovely,' she said as they marched over to their chosen spot. 'However did you find this place, David? It's so charming.'

They dug a hole, as per the instructions, and Edith placed the sapling in the ground. Then they sat on a park bench and watched it, imagining it fully grown and shading them from the sun. David had brought a packed lunch and they ate tuna fish sandwiches while the park around them gave birth to new trees. Then, as soon as she was finished her lunch, Edith stood up to walk away.

'I have to go home now,' she said, tears starting to come, her voice beginning to shake. 'I need to find my way home.'

'I'll take you, Edith,' David said. This wasn't her first time like this. 'Let me give you a ride.'

'You know the way, then?' she asked.

'Yes,' he said, as he had many times. 'Don't worry.'

*

Cathy walked through the new trees and headed to the colourful tents and flashing lights. David watched her from a few steps behind, wondering if he could leave her for a bit and lose himself in the trees. He wanted to find the one that he and Edith had planted, hoping that maybe it carried memories that even he had forgotten about. The park had changed. There was new play equipment, and the sandbox that had been in the corner was gone. David didn't know how to find his bearings. He realized that something so familiar could feel absolutely foreign.

'David,' Cathy said, turning. 'Are you all right?'

He didn't know how to answer that. In the beginning, when Edith first started to get sick, she would have moments of confusion, times when he would find her sitting, or standing, her forehead knitted as she tried to work out what she was doing, where she was going. And before he knew why she was confused, he would ask her, 'Are you all right?'

To which she always replied. 'I'm fine. Why shouldn't I be?'

So, as if conditioned, David prepared himself to answer Cathy in the same way. Only just as he thought he had the words, they stuck in his throat, bloated, and he couldn't get them out.

Cathy walked back to him and put her arm around his back. She leaned into his chest, but he barely felt her. He stood there wondering, since when, after all this time, had he been the one to get so confused?

'I'd like to go home,' she said, turning him away from the fairground, the flashing lights and all the screaming. 'Let's head back now.'

They didn't speak the whole way to the car and then only in short phrases on the way home. Cathy said she'd had a wonderful time. David said he was glad. Cathy said she would like to go back again, if and when he was up to it. David smiled at that and they both knew he didn't need to answer. After a while, she just looked out the window and when they passed by a herd of cows or a couple of horses she let out a sigh.

David dropped her off at home but couldn't look at her without the lump from the park still blocking his throat and everything he wanted to say.

She placed her hand on his knee. 'I know it's different now,' she said. 'But you'll see. We're all right.' Then she kissed his cheek and left.

David knew the route so well, he could drive it with his eyes closed. And although it was not that far from his house to the home, somehow, he never managed to walk it. This time he really wanted to get there quickly before they put her to bed.

Edith was sitting in the lounge area, watching *Jeopardy* with some of the other residents. One gentleman knew all of the answers for the category 'geography' and David wondered what he might have once been like at Trivial Pursuit. Edith watched silently, dressed in a pink tracksuit and a little bit of makeup – lipstick and blush that someone had put on for her that day. She always did prefer to wear makeup and David was glad that someone was remembering what she liked, even when she didn't.

'Hello, dear,' he said, pulling up a chair beside her. She looked over to him, not startled, but then she must be used to strangers coming up and sitting beside her. Thinking they knew her.

'Oh, hello,' she responded. She'd stopped addressing him by name long before she came to Tuxedo Villa and so he never expected her to remember him, not that that kept him from hoping.

'Your face is red,' she said and she reached a shaky hand out to touch David's nose, which was sunburnt despite Cathy's sunscreen.

'It was a lovely day, today,' he said.

'Yes, oh yes. I could . . . yes.'

'Edith,' David said, knowing he didn't have long, knowing she'd only let him beside her for a few minutes before she became agitated, confused, aware that she didn't know who he was. 'I've met a very nice woman.'

'Yes,' she said, quickly. 'They are.'

'Her name is Cathy and we've been spending a lot of time together.'

Edith turned her face back towards the television. She moved her lips as if reading the question along with the host.

'She's been taking very good care of me,' he said.

'That's good,' she said, and at first David thought it was more to the television than to him. Then she reached for his hand and placed it on her lap. She rubbed the skin of his palm without turning away from the screen, her body rocking slightly, her head nodding to all of the answers.

Polly Wright

POLLY WRIGHT is a lecturer, writer and actress. A founder member of the Birmingham-based Women and Theatre, she has co-written and performed in many plays and cabaret sketches. Polly runs Hearth, a centre for health, education and the humanities mediated through the arts. Her stories have been published in *Her Majesty*, *Going the Distance* and *Groundswell*.

Shropshire Gold
Polly Wright

Behind the dry cleaning covers and shoe rack, I find the box. At first I think it's one of Gran's hatboxes. But the shape's wrong. Square not oval. I plunge my hand to the back, jangling the coat hangers and tickling my nose with dust and mothballs, and pull it into the light.

It's the Russell and Bromley box. I open it slowly. It is lined with newspaper. That's funny, I can't remember doing that. But the newspapers are yellowy and old. Mum must have taken them out of their pink tissue paper and folded newspaper round and round them, as if they were broken glass to be disposed of sensibly.

The boots aren't white any more. More a dirty cream. The colour of newborn lambs, actually. In all the fairy tales and religious paintings their coats are snowy white – but they're wrong. Anyone who's lived on a farm can tell you how grubby they are.

I think it's a bit spooky I find the boots the same day as the anniversary. That's what I call it. Not *your* anniversary. That wouldn't be right. The anniversary.

In my witchy phase I'd have had an astrological explanation. Planets aligned and all that carry-on. I might drop in the shop in Bishop's Castle tomorrow to check my chart.

They've got all this fancy computer software that can tell you in an instant what's going on. Not that I believe it.

I take the boots out slowly and concentrate on them one at a time. Sounds stupid I know, but I sort of caress them. It's like they need the care they were never given. People should respect leather. In my veggie phase I wouldn't touch it. Just wore trainers and plastic. But I never stopped loving leather. I love its smell.

I put one boot to my face. Of course, the *new* smell has gone now. But there's no whiff of sweat either. I never really wore them, you see. Most of the time they just sat in the box they were bought in.

I think it's about time I told you a little bit more about my white boots.

I was younger than you are now when I went up to Town to get the boots. Some people round here call Shrewsbury Town. But people in the know, know that Town means London. The only place you could get boots like that was in Russell and Bromley's on Oxford Street.

I saw a picture of them in a magazine. Not a photo. A sort of line drawing. They were calf length and turned over at the top – with little cuts, the same shape you might make if you cut paper along the fold. Like diamonds.

But what made them so perfect was they were white. If you had the whole outfit, your dress would be white too. A short stiff boxy dress that was the height of cool. You still say *cool*, don't you? I've heard young people say that.

Everything white. White bag, white gloves, even white lipstick.

And the tights were very important. Shiny patterned tights, which I had the legs for.

As soon as I saw the boots, I had to have them. And I knew that Mum would never buy them for me. I was only fifteen. I couldn't get to London without my parents, and they hardly ever went there. Except once a year Mum went to see an old school friend and do some Christmas shopping. And she never took me. That was the one day out she had for herself, she used to say.

I saved up all my pocket money for months. Plus, I had a surprise windfall at Christmas. Mum and Dad gave me money to buy a tennis racket in the summer. That took it to the sum I needed. Including the return train fare.

Anyway, I planned my trip like I was getting out of Colditz. I heard this bloke Raymond talking in the butcher's about how he was taking some ewes Worcester way next Saturday. I saw him sneaking a glance as I went in the shop, so I knew he fancied me. You just know, don't you, when you're your age you have power over blokes. Specially sort of inadequate blokes like Ray.

So, the plan was: I'd meet him up at his dad's farm at some God-awful hour in the morning and he'd drop me off at Ludlow Station where I could catch a direct train to London. I knew that from Mum's Christmas day trips. Ray'd pick me up on his way back from Worcester. He'd have to hang around a bit, waiting for the train, but he seemed prepared to do that. S'pose he thought he was in with a chance of a snog. Well, he was really. The boots were worth a little sacrifice. I knew he wouldn't dare try anything heavy in case it got around. Everyone knew everyone in our village. No change there then.

My so-called friend Caro was my alibi. I told Mum and Dad I was going over to her place all day. I usually spent Saturdays with Caro anyway. Mostly we played Beatles records and tried out makeup in her room. But sometimes her mum let us go into Shrewsbury on the bus, so I got Caro to promise to say that that's what we were doing that Saturday. In case her mum blabbed to mine that I wasn't at her house.

Caro let me down in the end. Funny, even though it was so long ago, I never was friends with her again. I see her all the time. At the village supermarket, in the Duck, at the carnival. She's been married twice and between them her and Dave have got five kids. She always looks washed out. Hark at me, I can talk.

I often wondered why she did it. I think the truth was she didn't really like me. She was frightened of me.

Anyway, it all went like a dream until the end. I got the train and had a whole carriage to myself. I can remember it smelled of tobacco. I put my feet up on the seat opposite until I heard the guard coming, when I whipped them off. He gave me a funny look. I thought, perhaps he might know my dad.

London was pretty terrifying. All those people on the tube staring straight ahead, not registering your existence. I was glad they didn't see me, actually. I was wearing the coat Mum had got me at an outfitter's in Shrewsbury the year before. I had to have it because it was *good*. When Mum said *good* about clothes, it had a special meaning. It meant *expensive* and they would last a lifetime, whether you wanted them to or not.

On the train on the way back I locked myself in the loo to try the boots on. First – the tights. I stretched my legs out so I could admire the way the patterned nylon defined the curvy shape of my calves with that tiny hint of pattern, like it'd been traced on the nylon. Then – the boots. I put one foot up on the hand basin so I could see in the mirror how well they fitted. The lady in the shop had said, *It's as if they were made for you*, but they're told to say that, aren't they? I had to check for myself.

I bet you'd look good in them. Leather boots never go out of fashion, do they?

I imagine you're really pretty now. Dark curly hair. Elfin features. And splendid long legs which go on for ever. Just like mine.

I only came out of the loo when this woman banged on the door and shouted, *Are you all right in there?* And then she did one of those tutting, eyes-to-heaven jobs when I sauntered out right as rain. But what did I care what the old bag thought?

I stuffed the Russell and Bromley box in my duffle bag and went back to my carriage.

First person I saw when I got off the train was Dad. I could tell from the other end of the platform how upset he was. He had Raymond by the arm as if he was arresting him in a half-hearted sort of a way. Poor Raymond. He looked like he was crying. By the time I reached them Dad looked as if he might cry too. He was hopeless at discipline. Mum was the one that did all the grounding and stuff.

A few years ago I heard that Raymond had died. Farming accident, people said. But that often means suicide round here. He'd inherited his dad's farm and couldn't cope, so the story went. I felt sad for a long time when I heard that. I was a bitch to him and he was sweet, really. Thick. But sweet.

Mum never let me wear the white boots. They stayed in their box all those years, locked up in her wardrobe. But at some point she must have taken them out and humiliated them by wrapping them up in dirty newsprint.

I take the boots with me into my old bedroom. I click the latch and know exactly which floorboard will creak when I go over to the window. It's one of those gable windows that finishes so near the floor you can sit in it. Mum's put this posy of sweet peas there, which is nice of her. She doesn't usually bother.

I put the boots on the sill as if I'm letting them see what they've been missing. I bend my head and snuggle in beside them and look out at the garden and the familiar bounce and curve of the hills behind.

I remember having this argument with Kev once about what colour the distant hills were. He said they were turquoise and I said no, they were aquamarine. He said aquamarine was a poncy word like *eau de nil*, but I said it meant a sort of watery blue hence the *aqua* bit. I said I thought of Shropshire as that sort of blue.

He said he didn't. He thought of it as gold. He said it had the kind of light you get in those pictures of old England. You know the type; girls in bonnets sitting under oak trees looking at sheep. We were both out of our heads on mushroom brew, but afterwards I thought, he's right. Shropshire is gold.

Perhaps it's the anniversary, but this time of year makes me melancholy. Miserable, but sort of enjoying it? And I love the way every year things take you by surprise, although you know what's going to happen. The tight cream buds on the hawthorn bushes are like lace doilies. Soon the blossom will cover every bush like snow but just now, it's holding back.

There's this old hawthorn tree in the garden that's bent to the ground. When I was a kid I thought it was a woman. Like, frozen in time? The big branches were her arms over her head and the spiky twigs were her tangled hair. I told her stuff. Like what had gone on at school every day. Of course, when I was grounded after the London caboodle, she heard all about the white boots.

Last time I spoke to the tree was after what happened with you fifteen years ago. I'd come over and stayed the night with Mum and Dad because I couldn't stand it where I was living. I've lived in all sorts. Flats, houses, caravans, benders. I was in this gloomy old flat in Presteigne at the time. Tiny windows and chock full of heavy furniture. Anyway, I wanted to be at home, but I didn't want to tell

Mum and Dad what had happened. I said I had the flu and they didn't ask any questions.

So I stayed in my room and read my favourite books: *The Wind in the Willows*, *The Secret Garden* and *The Princess and the Goblin*. Dad brought me hot lemon drinks and even Mum knew to keep her distance. And one night there was a full moon and the light was silvery and ghostly. It had been raining and the wood of the hawthorn tree gleamed like iron. Well, I hadn't told anybody about you so I told the tree and I was crying and crying. In my head she told me it was OK. I'd done what was right for me. After that I started talking to you.

I know I should go down and help Mum with the tea. She's got this bloke coming round I think she's a bit sweet on. Not that she's told me. It's just the way she said his name: Donald Hutchinson. As if he was an actor or a politician and I should have heard of him.

I pop across the hallway and have a quick peep in Dad's study. It's tidier than usual with a funny, cloying sort of smell I can't place. My hackles rise. I don't like it, her going in there.

I run to the filing cabinet and pull it open. But nothing has changed. Buff folders peep out of wonky old hanging files. Full of letters from the bank in an old-fashioned type:

Dear Mr Forster,
   It is with great regret that we cannot agree to fund borrowing at such a level.

When I was a kid I used to sit in the corner of this room watching Dad write. I always had to be quiet till he'd finished. He'd press the paper on the blotter and fold it carefully before putting it in the envelope. Then he'd lick the gum slowly like he was eating an ice cream and crash his fist onto the flap to make it stick. I always wondered why he had to thump the envelopes like that. Mum just pressed them with her thumbs and it seemed to do the job just as well. After he'd gone to the post office I'd try to make out the mesh of words that had come through on the blotter. Sometimes there were whole phrases, but they were all jumbled up and didn't make much sense to me then. Collateral loan . . . Capital outlay . . . Substantial repayments . . .

Mum calls me down to give her a hand. I don't answer for a bit. I have to check that nothing in the files has been moved without asking me. But it's still all there. The file of my letters to him after I left home. Another for my birth certificate with a photo slipped in that I'd never seen until after he died. Him holding me as a baby, wrapped up in a shawl. We're sitting on the combine when it was all shiny and new. He's grinning at the person taking the photo as if his face might split. Perhaps someone else took it. I never remember him smiling like that at her.

Then I work out what that smell is. Bloody *air freshener*! Mum's gone mad on air freshener recently since she found out about it from her mate Mildred. Mildred's letting out some of her rooms for B&B and she's told Mum how lovely and fresh this pine forest is and how it can get rid of all the fusty damp smells of old houses. Well, I can just about put up with it in the toilet but not here in his study. Where it still smells of him.

I think about the flowers in my bedroom and I think about Donald.

Mum calls 'Ann!' sharply this time and I say, 'Coming.' I look in my room on the way downstairs and decide to leave the boots on the windowsill by the sweet peas. To give her a start.

Mum's in the kitchen, cutting the crust off bread to make delicate sandwiches. Not many people serve up sandwiches for tea now, but Mum's a traditionalist. She doesn't trust me to slice the cucumber thin enough, so I get the job of arranging cakes on the plate. She's ashamed they're shop cakes, but she's never been a great one for home baking and it's been a while since the last WI stall.

I catch her staring at me while I'm unwrapping the mini chocolate swiss rolls.

I say 'What?' and she says, 'That's a nice top, dear.' But I know that's not what she's thinking. She's thinking I look a mess. Mum keeps up standards in the clothes department. She's wearing her pleated skirt and Aran cardigan and paisley green and cream scarf tied in a knot. Her shoes are very *good*. Rounded court design with a blocky sort of heel in rich tan. She's had them for years, but they've kept their shape. Mum's a great advert for the shoetree.

The bell goes and she still hasn't finished the sandwiches, let alone powdered her nose and I have to open the door. This old chap is standing there in his green raincoat and brogues, leaning on one of the sticks we sell at Merlin's Grove.

'So, you must be the daughter,' he says.

I stifle the urge to say, 'So, you must be the boyfriend,' because he isn't yet and Mum would be mortified. I'm polite as anything and say, 'Donald, isn't it?' and offer to hang up his coat.

Mum comes bustling into the porch and whisks him away to show him the garden. I think she's worried what I might say to him, and I wonder why she's bothered to ask me over. Then I realize that I'm a chaperone. It might have seemed a bit forward to invite him round to tea on his own. I look out of the big bay window at him following Mum round the flower beds with his hands clasped behind his back and I think of Dad sweating his guts out digging and pruning and composting just so she can impress some other man.

I start saying Dad's phrases in my head: 'What's your game, feller-my-lad? Eh? Eh? Mister?' as if he's talking through me.

They come back in and we all sit down to tea. For a moment the only sounds are the chink of china and a bit of tea-slurping from Donald. Mum won't like that, I think, but when I look at her she seems to be grinning all over her chops. I look at Donald and I can sort of see he might be a bit of a catch. He's got one of those bony faces with good skin the colour of russet apples. And a loud, posh voice as if he's lord of the bloody manor or something. Probably supports the hunt.

He's telling us about his younger daughter who's just got married.

'What does her husband do?' Mum hasn't twigged that you don't ask that any more. But old Donald doesn't mind. Gets stuck in.

'Senior Partner in one of the oldest legal firms in London. Youngest they've taken on at that level in years. Heading for the Bench at this rate.'

'You must be thrilled,' Mum simpers.

'They told Marjorie they were getting engaged before she died.' I wonder how recently that was. Merry Widower meets Merry Widow.

'How lovely.'

'Wonderful spring wedding. All their legal friends there. She's a barrister, you see.'

'Who?'

'Harriet. My daughter.'

'Goodness! A barrister! How marvellous.'

I'm thinking, I want to get out of here. I want to be sitting in the Duck with a pint and a rollie.

'Look. This was taken when she was called to the Bar.' He gets out a picture of Harriet in her robes.

'Ooh. Isn't she pretty? Look, Ann. Isn't she lovely?'

I nod. It's one of those well-lit studio set-ups, which can hide a multitude of horrors, but you can tell Harriet is good looking in a Sloaney sort of way.

I say, 'I think you and I have met before, Donald.'

He looks a bit nonplussed and says, 'Have we? I'm sorry, my memory's not what it was.'

'Weren't you at the Meet in the village square? On New Year's Day? I'm sure I saw you on a horse.'

'Oh no, my dear. It certainly wasn't me. I'm opposed to hunting.' I look at Mum. She's dead in favour. We've had loads of run-ins about animal rights.

But she says, smooth as butter, 'It is rather cruel, I agree.'

I can't let this pass. '*You've* changed your tune.'

'A lady's entitled to change her mind, Ann. It is a free country.'

'Maybe we've met at the shop,' Donald goes on.

'Oh. Have you come into Merlin's Grove? Did we sell you your stick?'

He looks bemused again. He's got a good line in bemused.

'He means *his* shop, Ann. Donald's got a shop in Town. Antique books.'

'Second-hand?' I say.

'More rare books. First editions, that sort of thing,' he says genially.

I nod at our shelves, buckling slightly under the strain of all the books Dad collected over the years.

'I hope you're not after Mum for her books. First editions are ten a penny in our house.'

'Ann!'

It's unforgivable, I know. Donald's healthy glow turns puce and Mum looks as if she's going to kill me. Or at the very least send her middle-aged daughter to her room.

'I'm sorry. Just a joke. In appalling taste, I know. Forgive me,' I say and head out to the garden.

I sit by Dad's rockery and open my Golden Virginia tin. I roll three fags and smoke them all. I'm usually good at rolling, but today my hands shake so much the ciggies are too loose and I have to pull strands of tobacco off my lower lip. It starts to rain.

After a while, Mum comes out. She knows we're going to have a row but she's bothered to put her raincoat and outdoor shoes on first.

'What's got into you?'

'I found the boots,' I say.

'What boots?'

'The boots. My white Russell and Bromley boots. You kept them in the cupboard all that time.'

'Ann. What in God's name are you talking about?'

'You know. Why did it matter so much? Was it that I lied, or was it that you didn't like how *sexy* they made me look?'

'Oh. Those boots.' She sits down on Dad's favourite rock.

'You were jealous, weren't you?'

'Don't be ridiculous.'

'Because I might be having fun.'

'You were *fifteen*, Ann!'

'You hated sex with Dad, so you took it out on me. All that free love in the sixties. God, I bet you hated that.' I feel dizzy and light-headed. I feel like I can say anything. I might even tell her about the anniversary. I want to tell her it was her fault, although I know it wasn't.

She's not looking at me at all.

'And now you're *dancing* on Dad's grave.' Her whole body is turned away from me now. I notice that her back is getting that old woman's hump.

'He's only been dead a year,' I say. But I can't muster any anger now, so it comes out a bit feeble.

She looks at me at last, her face sagging beneath orange powder. She says, 'Maybe, Ann, I'm having a little bit of fun.'

Through the window I see Donald pouring himself another cup of tea. Even from this distance, I can see the pot is shaking so much he has to use his other hand to steady it.

Mum's voice is firm. 'Ann. When are you going to stop blaming me for what you haven't done with your life?'

I pick up my tobacco tin and get the hell out.

In the Duck, Rick, the barman, persuades me to try the latest brew.

'You're looking a bit peaky, my love. See if this puts hair on your chest.'

'I hope not, Rick,' I say in a flirty tone.

He says, 'Let me know if you think it's too hoppy.'

I'm noticing that about men. When you're past the first flush, as it were, they treat you differently. They're polite and friendly, but it's as if you're more a mate than a woman.

I sit in the snug, and rest my cheek against the smooth oak. I roll another fag and get the brew down as fast as possible.

Then you walk in.

You stand for a moment in the middle of the pub. You're looking for someone. Your eyes move from the old blokes in the corner playing dominoes, to the barman, to the jukebox, to me.

There you are. Elfin features, brown eyes. Tangled hair. From where I'm sitting, I could lean over and put my fingers in your ringlets right up to your scalp.

You look at me without really seeing me. As if I'm a ghost.

Rick says, 'Are you looking for your dad, love?'

You nod.

'He usually comes in a bit later, love. Is it urgent? Can I give him a message?'

'Yeah.' And you go over and tell him something and then go.

Except it's not you. Because you don't exist.

I remember every detail of that place. Gravel drive. Huge copper beeches. Hallway smelling of polish. They took me to a poky room and asked me to pay up front. I counted out the notes like they do at the bank.

They asked if I was married and how old I was. I said no to the first question and twenty-eight to the second. The doctor was quite kind. He asked me had I thought about it enough. Having an illegitimate child wasn't a crime any more. In my head I replay it. I say, 'You're right, doctor.' And get up and leave. I've done it so often I nearly believe it.

But I didn't say anything. I just wanted them to get on with it. To feel myself again.

I still believe in a woman's right and all that.

It's just I keep seeing you. What you would have been like. I still hang out with Kev in the Duck. And now I've seen his grown-up daughter.

But not mine.

Kev'll probably be in, in a minute. Like Rick says, he usually drops off for a pint on his way back from work. He won't be surprised to see me; I'm often in here. Maybe I'm gearing up for my alcoholic phase.

Kev's a good mate now. In a way he always was. He wasn't like my great love. I've had one of them and I know the difference. I never told Kev about what I did. We only went to bed together a couple of times. It was in my magic mushroom phase and, to be honest, most of the time we were too out of it to get it together properly. Usually we ended up laughing and having stupid conversations.

If I'd said I was, you know, pregnant, it would have turned it into something else. Something it wasn't. He might have thought I was pressurizing him to leave his wife, or pay up. It would have been, well, embarrassing.

He can buy me a drink when he comes in. I don't trust my voice enough to go up to the bar. I'm not in the mood for banter.

If Kev doesn't have to rush home tonight, we'll try a few of the local brews together: Butty Bach, Dorothy Goodbody's, Draught Worthington, John Roberts XXX.

Shropshire Gold.

And you never know, I might get so slaughtered I tell him.

Finding Alteration
Polly Wright

Since Tony left it had been Alice's job to pick up the post and the newspaper from the doormat. She handed Ruth the letter and then stood at the breakfast bar in her short shiny skirt, her headphones on, thumb jabbing at her mobile as she pushed the white-bread toast and black-currant jam into her mouth.

After all these years Ruth knew the cramped spiky handwriting. She stared at the envelope so intensely even Alice noticed.

'You OK, Mum?'

When Alice was putting the milk back in the fridge (amazingly, without being asked), Ruth tore the envelope open and, seeing his signature, pushed it under the news-paper. Whatever was in it, she didn't want Alice to witness her reading it.

On her way to work, Ruth parked the car in a street she'd never been down before. She sat for a moment and watched clumps of kids dawdling to school. A few of the older ones were lighting cigarettes behind bushes, and stamping their feet in the cold. One girl walked on her own, eyes down. Once, when Alice was little, Ruth had observed her on her own like that in the playground.

Stoke Newington,
N16.

Dear Ruth,

What can I say? Thirty years on!!

At a conference last month (on Urban Regeneration –
for my sins) I ran into Simon Cotterill, would you
believe? I saw his name on the delegate list and wondered
vaguely if it was our esteemed Head Boy – and then he
stood up and gave a presentation on partnerships in the
Black Country. Instantly I was back in the school hall,
with old Simon strutting his Debating Soc stuff. I'd never
have recognized him. He's got even less hair than I have!
Frankly, I was surprised he wasn't the obligatory Minister
they send to these events. He's pure New Labour.

I digress – as always. I tracked him down afterwards
and we caught up on old times. Well, you came up, and
he said you still live in the Midlands and your paths cross
at work! As luck would have it, he had your home address
in his state-of-the-art organizer. He told me you're the
secretary for some Voluntary Sector committee he chairs.

Next time I'm in Brum would you mind if I looked you
up? I hear they've knocked down the Bull Ring and the
old place is unrecognizable. Be my guide.

Hope you're well and all that,

Yours,

Dan (Toberman)

PS Simon said you have a teenage daughter. I've got
three kids – two girls and a boy.

Ruth folded the letter slowly and put it back in the envelope. She knew the whole thing by heart already, but she
needed to keep it – she'd want to look at it later to check
she'd got things right. She pushed it into one of the back
pockets of her bag where you were meant to keep loose
change, and zipped it up.

She remembered the hall in the boys' school. Every year
they invited sixth-formers from the girls' school to be in

their play. That year it was *Serjeant Musgrave's Dance*. She remembered running back into the hall one evening after rehearsal because she'd forgotten her script. She knew she'd left it in the wings, but it was getting dark and she didn't know how to turn the stage lights on. She went up the stage steps hesitantly and felt her way along the curtains to find the opening. She recalled the fusty smell of the heavy material and how the feel of the fabric set her teeth on edge.

She suddenly sensed that there was someone backstage. She called out and was embarrassed by the tremor in her voice.

'Who is it?'

Dan's pale face hung like a mask as he peeped through the gap in the curtains.

'I wanted to talk to you.'

'You scared me.'

'I love you.'

She remembered shaking on the edge of the stage. Dan was playing Serjeant Musgrave himself. His floppy brown hair fell over his blue eyes. Everyone at her school fancied him. And he was telling *her* he loved *her*.

Now the kids were running towards the school gate. One little boy lolloped over the crossing, his heavy bag knocking against his legs and unbalancing him. The smokers stubbed out their fags, self-consciously grinding them into the dirt.

Be my guide. Was that a reference? Although they'd been at separate schools, she and Dan had done the same A-level syllabus. They used to parody their set books. Arms out. Eyes shut. Old man tremor. 'Be my guide, Jane,' Blind Rochester to Jane Eyre. She spoke her reply now as she watched the lollipop lady beckon the last stragglers across the road. *Sir, I am the apple of your eye.*

One time, Dan had recited a whole Shakespeare sonnet to her when they were sitting in a transport café in Digbeth. She remembered blushing so much her ears tingled and she wondered if she might swoon and if that was what the word *swoon* meant: to pass out with sheer emotion. He didn't touch her while he spoke the poem. Just held her with his blue eyes. She couldn't recall which sonnet it was, but she could remember what she had written in her diary: *His eyes are like the sea.*

She thought about the gaps. No mention of his wife – or her husband. But he knew, he must know, about Tony leaving. Simon would have told him. His marriage must have finished or he wouldn't be writing, would he? She watched a woman throw a stick for a dog in the park opposite the school, her cream raincoat billowing. Idly she recognized the mac as Marks and Spencer. She had the navy version. The dog bounded and leapt, barking hysterically in the wind. Crows flapped in the scribble of high branches. Ruth embraced the steering wheel and rested her head on the top. Feeling the cold plastic against her cheek, she gave way to a moment of pure joy.

A phone call at work later that day confirmed that Dan's marriage had ended. Ruth had known Simon Cotterill as long as Dan, but had never liked him, and cared little about his opinion of her. All the same, she felt obliged to concoct a reason for ringing him and that proved easy enough. She suggested a minor additional item for the agenda of the next Joint Strategic Partnership meeting to her manager, and offered to ring the Chair. Jenny, who disliked Simon as much as Ruth did, agreed gratefully.

Ruth was diplomatic about the proposed item and amenable to Simon's insistence that it be relegated to AOB.

Her hand sweated round the receiver. She could feel the warmth of her breath in the mouthpiece.

'I hear you met Daniel Toberman.'

'Dan? Oh, yes. Padded out a bit, but still the same old Dan. Works for one of the London PCTs now. Nothing special – not a director. With his degree you'd have thought he'd have done better. Wife's left him. You could tell. Shirt wasn't ironed. Sorry. Joke. Ruth? Anyway, he wanted to know all about you. Old boyfriend of yours, wasn't he?'

'Have you got his e-mail address, Simon? Only we're doing a national seminar around sharing good practice with PCTs. It might be useful to have some more delegates from London on board.' Her voice was flinty, repelling the familiarity of Simon's tone.

E-mail was easier, she thought. Not as special as letters.

Hi Dan,
Great to hear from you! Thirty years? Is it really that long? Do you still kiss like a dream and are your eyes still like the sea? DELETE

Hello Dan,
Thank you for your letter. Incredible to hear from you after such a long time. I doubt if you would recognize me nowadays! The years have taken their toll. Yes, it would be lovely to see you. DELETE

Dear Dan,
Well, your letter was a surprise. Yes – I work for the Voluntary Sector Council now. I understand from Simon that you might be interested in our joint working strategy. We're planning a seminar and we need more representatives from the London boroughs. I wondered – would you like to be a delegate?

She went to find Jenny, who was anxiously scrutinizing plans for the New Build.

'I've got another London delegate for the Sharing Good Practice seminar. London. Stoke Newington, or thereabouts.'

'Oh. Great,' said Jenny vaguely, turning the plan the other way up.

That day, Ruth popped into Sainsbury's after work and bought herself treats. Varnished emerald avocados, round and heavy with just the right squashiness at the tips. Cellophane-packed French beans in tidy rows. Salmon en Croûte with a luscious picture of flaky pastry and bright pink fish on its cardboard packaging. Chicken Massala and Lamb Passanda with tall tubs of saffron rice, flecked with black peppercorns. Pasta parcels stuffed with wild mushrooms, tomatoes and mozzarella.

Oh, yeah, she could hear Tony saying. *How many chemicals are there in all that?* Tony couldn't bear anything that wasn't natural, that smacked of convenience foods. When they'd first got married she'd admitted to him that she didn't like cooking and he was all forgiving then. Said it didn't matter. But a few years into their marriage he started giving her recipe books for Christmas. He tried to be a role model and cooked elaborate meals at weekends. He'd pick the hardest recipes from Elizabeth David and take all afternoon to make rough puff pastry and set things in gelatine. He'd marinate the meat and let the onions sweat. But that lowered her confidence so much so that she became dangerously bad. She burned things and turned the fan on, desperate to get rid of the smell. She threw ruined pans straight in the dustbin, sometimes plunging her hands into the rubbish to make sure they were well covered before running to the hardware shop to replace them. But he always noticed. The ones she bought weren't non-stick or they were aluminium or they didn't have wooden handles. When, at their last Christmas together, he viciously gave her *Delia's How to Cook* she gave up altogether and they started to eat separately.

When she got home with her heavy Sainsbury's bags, she didn't even sit down for a cup of tea. She warded off the emptiness by cleaning the house. She crashed the vacuum cleaner out of the cupboard and set its high whine going, clattering into corners, its hollow plastic finger sucking up the velvet curtains. She turned on Radio 2, defiantly as if willing Tony to come in and turn it back to Radio 4. As she was bending over the toilet, turning the water turquoise and singing along with Sting, she became aware that Alice was standing in the doorframe.

'Mum, are you all right?' Her voice sounded friendly, like the old Alice, and when Ruth sat back on her heels and looked at her she saw that she was laughing. Ruth realized she hadn't seen Alice laugh for a long time.

'Like you're singing to yourself, Mum,' she said, as if it was unusual. Ruth always sang along to the radio and when Alice was a little girl they both did.

'Good day, love?' Ruth asked.

'Yeah. Sorry I'm late.'

Ruth tried not to show her shock at hearing the word *sorry*.

'I was meeting Jo.'

'Who's she, love?'

'She's a *he*, Mum. He's asked me out.'

Ruth looked away. Alice was far too young. She wasn't doing well in her schoolwork and a boyfriend would be bound to affect her GCSEs. But Alice might be in love just like Ruth had been when she was at school. And Tony would hate it that Alice had a boyfriend. Turning to her daughter, she saw herself – not Tony, whom Alice really resembled – and tenderness flooded her.

'Is he nice?'

'Yeah, Mum. Look.' She flicked her silver phone open and handed it to her. Ruth groped for her glasses to scrutinize the gaudy image on the screen.

'Lovely,' she said, staring at the boy's face.

Today really has been perfect, Ruth thought at dinner as

she watched Alice eat whole mouthfuls of the Salmon en Croûte. She listened indulgently to Alice's descriptions of Joe and how he'd told a friend that he thought Alice was a *babe*. Ruth remembered Alice on her own that day in the playground and she felt a thrill of fear and pride. She was part of the game now.

A few days later, Dan rang her at work. She had spent a few fretful days regretting her e-mail to him. Was her rapid response unseemly? Should she have held back? Life probably hadn't changed that much – women didn't approach men now any more than they did when they were young. But she hadn't approached him. He had written her a letter, she kept telling herself as none of her phones rang. Home. Work. Mobile. Silence can shroud a phone. She became tense, alert to the silence wherever she was.

Alarmingly, she found herself drifting off at meetings. She had a reputation as an excellent chair and prided herself on being able to manage people considered by others to be impossible. But since the letter, her memories of Dan's kisses were so strong that the old swoony feeling overcame her and she let people ramble and become irrelevant.

Ruth loved her job. She had never really expected to have a career and joined the organization as a volunteer, needing something to get her out of the house. But she was so efficient they'd offered her a paid position almost immediately. And after Tony had walked out on he she'd proved herself so invaluable that now she was being groomed for senior management. She couldn't afford to falter.

When Dan phoned she had genuinely forgotten about him. She and Jenny were bent towards her computer, studying a spreadsheet as they planned the seminar. Jenny was a large, distracted woman who had been promoted above her competence and she easily became defensive if she felt insecure. Ruth worked hard at not threatening her. Recently they had started confiding in each other, bemoaning their lack of men, their sudden and embarrassing desire for sex. But Ruth hadn't confided about Dan.

Ruth picked up the phone. 'Ruth Shaker.'

'Hello, Ruthie!'

'Sorry?'

'Ruthie! Don't you get called that any more?'

'Oh, I'm sorry. Is that Dan?' Ruth's hand went up to her neck and fiddled with her gold chain. Jenny went on stolidly frowning at the computer screen, but her whole body was listening.

'Sorry I didn't phone you before – I've only just got a window. As we say in the twenty-first century.'

'Oh no, not at all.' Not at all what? she thought. 'It's just that I'm in a meeting right now.'

'Look, I'll be quick. Why don't we meet up? Go for a meal or something?' Ruth looked at Jenny's broad back.

'That would be nice.' She wondered how such an arrangement was going to be accomplished. He hardly lived down the road.

'I thought I might come up to the auld counteree,' he said in a Scottish accent.

'Sorry?'

'You know, frequent our old haunts, go down Memory Lane!'

She felt hot with unease. Try as she might she couldn't detect the young Dan in his voice. The Midlands accent had gone and he seemed bluff and jocular. As if he had cast their whole relationship as a *laugh*.

'Yes, that would be nice,' she said again. 'How about the seminar?'

'No, can't make that. Sorry.'

'Oh.'

'How about Saturday? The twenty-eighth. When I don't have the kids?'

And where would he stay? she panicked. Alice was going to Tony's that weekend. That meant the house would be empty and sex would be an option.

'And would you stay with your parents?'

'My folks? Oh no, Ruthie, I'm afraid they're long dead.'

'Oh, God, I'm sorry.'

'No worries. They died ages ago. No – I'll have to stay with you, Ruthie. If that's *OK*.'

'OK,' she said slowly. Perhaps I can give Tony a weekend off, she thought. Alice can be my chaperone. Jenny had given up all pretence of working and was smirking at her. She had to ring off. 'Look, Dan, I'm sorry, I'm going to have to go. I am in the middle of a meeting.'

'Sorry, Ruthie. It's lovely to hear your voice.'

'Yes,' she said stiffly.

'Give me your home number. I'll give you a bell tonight.'

'I'll give you my mobile.' She didn't want Alice answering the phone to him. Then she added stiffly, 'It's lovely to hear from you,' in case she was appearing unfriendly and would regret it later.

As she put the phone down, Jenny's smirk turned into a wide grin. 'So? Who was it lovely to hear from?' she asked.

Ruth looked at her watch. 'We'd better get this done before we go home.'

The cinema was warm. Too warm for Ruth, who was having hot flushes. But she didn't mind. She was enjoying the closeness with Alice. It was raining out and their wet coats smelled like straw. They leaned towards each other, their heads almost touching as they shared an ice cream and stared up at the screen. Alice had wanted to see the film because she said Joe looked like Jude Law. Ruth found this difficult to believe, but she pretended she saw what Alice meant. Ruth liked Jude Law too, although Alice told her, 'Hands off, cradle-snatcher. Stick to Nicole Kidman's father.' Ruth studied Donald Sutherland and practised fancying him.

After the film they hung around in the new Bullring and stared at the displays of huge cut-outs of young people – perfectly beautiful as they strode towards some immaculate future. In a gap between the brilliant shop windows a pale church spire cut modestly into the watery night sky.

Alice linked her arm in Ruth's and rubbed her face on her shoulder like she used to do when she was younger. Ruth took a deep breath.

'You know – the weekend of the twenty-eighth? When you're going to stay with Dad?'

'Yeah.'

'Well, I wondered. If you could go and see him this weekend instead. An old friend's coming to visit me and I'd like you to meet him.'

'What old friend?'

'His name's . . .' She took another breath. Nerves trapped her. 'His name's Dan. And. Well, he's coming to Birmingham. For a conference. And he wanted to. Pop in.'

'And stay the night?'

'Well, yes.' Alice took her arm away. 'He lives in London . . .' Ruth trailed off. 'Is it OK? Ali?'

'Whatever.'

They walked for a while in silence. Boys in baggy T-shirts and baseball caps circled around them on skateboards.

'Look. The shops are still open. Shall we have a look?' Ruth knew Alice wanted a new top.

'Whatever.'

In New Look Alice tried on a plastic bow covered in gold glitter. She put her head on one side and pirouetted at her reflection in the mirror. 'Very *bling bling*!' she said.

'What does that mean?'

Alice shrugged. 'Nothing.' She flicked through clothes on a circular rail. 'Mum. Did you love Dad when you married him?'

'Yes, I think so.'

'You *think* so!'

'Yes, I did love him. Of course I did.'

Alice swung a pink top hung with silver chains off the rail. 'I'm going to try this on.'

'D'you want me to come in with you?'

'No.'

When she came back from the changing rooms, Ruth was gazing at a strappy dress of blue, pink and purple sequins. She held it up against her. 'What d'you think I'd look like in this?'

'Fat.' Ruth looked at Alice. 'Sorry, Mum. You have to be really skinny to wear a dress like that.'

Ruth didn't speak for a while, all traces of the companionable warmth gone. She hadn't really got used to her middle-aged body. When she was young, her friends had called her Twiggy. Her favourite outfit had been a ribbed jumper, a hipster miniskirt and knee-high leather boots. *You wait*, she silently addressed her daughter.

On the bus home, Ruth said, 'I suppose I should go to the gym, shouldn't I?'

Alice put her head in her arms on the metal rail of the seat in front. She kicked at the discarded bus tickets and said nothing.

'Perhaps we could go together.'

'Mu-um.' Alice groaned and kicked the floor harder.

'Stop doing that.' Ruth snapped.

The bus swayed as it went round the new Selfridges building. A great curvaceous fish with shining silver scales. Ruth turned to Alice, wanting to share it. But Alice was slumped in her seat, punching at her mobile.

*

The best bit about going to the gym was coming home, Ruth thought. She spent longer under the shower than usual, stretching her neck towards the spray like a supplicant. In her bedroom afterwards, she took the Chinese dressing gown Tony had brought back for her after one of his business trips out of the wardrobe. She'd refused to wear it, knowing that it needed more than a bit of silk to revive their sex life. Now she put it on, and felt it cling to her warm damp body.

Alice wasn't home yet so she was able to play her favourite music. She put on Fleetwood Mac as loud as she dared and lay on the bed, raising herself every now and then to take delicious sips of gin and tonic.

She remembered Dan taking her into the changing rooms at the boys' school one evening when neither of them was wanted for rehearsal. She was shocked by the sheer stink and disorder of men. Rank football shirts. Fungal socks. Discarded boots lolling rudely, tongues askew.

He led her by the hand to the slatted bench and cupped her face in his hands. Like Richard Burton and Elizabeth Taylor in *Cleopatra*. They kissed and kissed while she breathed in the foxy smell.

She imagined him now, on the bed, kissing her, and feeling her body through the slippery fabric. She didn't bother with the details of how he'd got into the bedroom, what had happened to Alice, or how she'd got out of her clothes and into the dressing gown. She whispered: *I have always loved you. We were meant to be together, you are more beautiful than I remember you . . .*

She didn't hear the door open, so it was a while before she became aware of Alice's presence in the room. She sat up, too quickly, and the gin rushed to her head.

'Darling. You're back.'

'I know who Dan is. He was your boyfriend when you were at school, wasn't he? Dad told me you always went on about Dan being your *first love*.' She sneered the last words.

'He was my first boyfriend, yes. But he's a friend now. I wanted you to meet him.' Ruth felt her stomach fall away as she tried to meet her daughter's stare.

'D'you think I'm going to stay here while you have sex with him?'

'I wasn't going to.'

'That's why you're going to the gym, though, isn't it? So he'll want to have sex with you. Isn't it?'

'No!'

'Like, what are you wearing, Mum?'

Ruth looked down at the pink dragons as if she too had forgotten what she had on.

'God, it's disgusting. I don't want to listen to you shagging in the next-door room.'

'Alice!'

'Anyway, I've arranged with Dad. I'm going to his place. *That* weekend.'

She slammed the door so hard that the whole flimsy house seemed to shudder.

Three weeks later Ruth lay on her bed and watched the digits change on her clock. In an hour Dan would be here, but she felt paralysed with dread. She stared at the frieze round the edge of the bedroom wall. On a pale blue background, which matched the duvet perfectly, androgynous pink men on long legs pulled at bows and arrows. She'd bought it after she and Tony had split up – as if to spite him, even though she knew he'd never see it. At the same time, she'd also bought a bed with drawers underneath the mattress, where you could store your shoes and things. The drawers were white, with gold handles. Now she saw it all through Dan's eyes, remembering him laughing hysterically about the bourgeois dressing table in her mother's room. She resolved again that he wasn't going to see her bedroom.

Ruth remembered visiting Verulaneum when she was a child. She'd cried when she got home because it had just been a few old stones, not the Roman city of her picture book. As a teenager she'd felt the same disappointment when she tasted asparagus and found, not a delicacy, but a thready bit of slime. As she'd grown older, she'd schooled herself to expect less. Now, lying on the bed, she ticked herself off for letting down her guard.

Eventually, she got up and laid out her new bra and matching knickers on the bed, the lace like crimson filigree. After she'd accepted that Alice was not going to be at home, a little element of *just in case* had crept into her preparations. After agreeing to some extra highlights at the hairdresser's, she went upstairs to the beautician's for a leg wax, which she usually only afforded herself when she was going on holiday. And while she was there, she thought she might as well have a pedicure and her toenails painted in mother-of-pearl varnish. On her way home she'd been enticed into a fancy underwear shop that she'd never noticed before.

Now she stared grimly at her reflection in the mirror. She wouldn't normally tolerate this view of herself, letting the cruel evening sunlight expose her crumpled neck. She dug her fingers into her flesh, lifting it up, wishing she could iron the skin smooth and tight.

She went into the bathroom. Bottles stood on the four corners of the bath like purple and orange sentinels. Nivea, cotton wool and skin toner waited in the basket. What had felt like an anointing ritual now seemed tacky. Very *bling bling*, she heard Alice say and she longed for her to be here. The empty house hurt her ears. As she walked around it, she hated the insistent monotone of the fridge. The sudden whirr and clatter of the fan in the downstairs toilet.

I have always loved you. Now she knew she couldn't possibly say anything of the kind. It was the sort of thing you said when you were young, when you were trying romantic phrases out. You didn't have to mean them. But now she couldn't bear to take such a risk. She was terrified she might have already given herself away – and she sieved all the words she had spoken to him since his letter for hints of expectation.

When she opened the door, an old man stood looking at her. He was almost completely bald and a wisp of his surviving hair stood ludicrously on end.

'Hi. It's Dan.'

'Yes,' she said. 'Yes. I know.'

'You didn't think I'd come, did you?'

'Of course I did. Well.' She held onto the doorframe.

'Aren't you going to ask me in?'

'You look great,' he said later, sloshing red wine into his glass. He placed the bottle close to him, as if someone might take it off him. 'You haven't changed at all.'

Ruth half twisted her body round to check who was at the table behind her without seeming too obvious. Recently the owners had replaced the carpets and thick wallpaper with white walls and a beech floor so it looked more like an art gallery than a restaurant. You could hear what everyone was saying as clearly as if you were sharing a front room with them. And Dan was talking loudly.

'Oh, come on!' she said heartily.

'No. Honestly, Ruthie. If anything you're even more gorgeous. God, how we all lusted after you at school.'

She hated to admit it, but Simon Cotterill was right. It *was* obvious that Dan's wife had left him. His orange shirt clashed with his brown trousers and the corner of his collar wouldn't lie flat. His skin was pasty and she suspected he lived on takeaways.

'Do you ever see anyone from school these days? Apart from Simon?'

'Well, I used to see a lot of Sally, of course. At university.'

'Oh yes?' Dan had chucked Ruth for Sally, who'd played Annie, at the cast party after the last performance of *Serjeant Musgrave's Dance*. *My life is not worth living*, she remembered writing in her diary.

'Sorry about Sally, Ruthie.' He grinned at her, boyishly.

'It was a long time ago, Dan.'

He tore off a piece of nan bread and rolled it round in his Chicken Dhansak.

'Indian people eat it like this, don't they?' he said.

She watched as the crimson sauce dripped onto his shirt front, like blood. She wondered if she should point it out.

'Excuse me! Over here! Another red.' Dan waved the empty wine bottle at the waiter as if it were a visual aid.

She and Tony had come to this restaurant for years, and after he'd left her, Ruth had introduced Jenny to it too. She knew the waiters by name and often saw the women of the family in Sainsbury's or on the high street with their kids.

'Thank you, Ranjit.' She smiled and tried to catch his eye when he came over, wanting to disassociate herself from Dan's behaviour. She put her hand over her own glass.

'First-name terms?' Dan asked.

'I often come here after work with my boss.'

'*Say no more*, Ruthie! D'you remember *say no more?*' He used a Cockney accent and gave a heavy stage wink.

She remembered how all the girls used to stand around laughing while the boys repeated phrases in regional accents. They weren't really that funny, she thought.

'My boss is a woman,' she said sharply.

'Sorry.' Dan tried to focus. 'So – what's your position? At the VSC?'

'Assistant Manager.'

'That's really good, Ruthie.' His patronizing tone stung her.

'I've been asked to go for Equalities Lead.'

'Wow,' he said.

They both shifted their eyes away to watch a young woman in a miniskirt walk the length of the room. Ruth thought about Alice and wondered how she was getting on with Tony.

'So what d'you think of the Green Paper on Social Exclusion?' he asked.

'I only skimmed it. What do you think?'

'Typical New Labour. More meaningless targets.'

She'd been impressed by the Green Paper, but hadn't the heart to argue. She let him talk while her attention drifted off to the Tenants' Association meeting she had to chair the following week.

'That's very interesting. I hadn't thought of it that way,' she said when he stopped talking.

'Sorry. Gone on, haven't I? Bit of a hobby horse of mine.' He gulped another mouthful of wine and stared at the girl in the miniskirt who was now standing a few feet away from them.

'D'you know that girl?' Ruth asked.

Dan dropped his gaze guiltily. 'No, of course not. I haven't lived here for thirty years. She's just, well –'

'Lovely?'

'I suppose she is a bit of a babe.'

'Babe?' The word on his lips made her squirm. She could see why Alice didn't want to tell her what *bling bling* meant.

'She reminds me of you, Ruthie. When you were that age.'

'Ruth, Dan. My name is Ruth. Nobody calls me Ruthie any more.' Her own vehemence took her by surprise.

'I'm sorry, Ruthie, *Ruth*.' His eyes had that same punched, hurt look she remembered from the school hall. As if he was asking her to take responsibility for arousing strong feelings in him.

There was a silence while Dan's wayward strands of hair quivered. Ruth poured more wine into her glass so roughly she spilt some on the tablecloth.

'Shit,' she said, rubbing at the pink stain.

When the bill came, Dan crowed, 'After Eights. Far out! D'you remember *far out*, Ruthie – sorry, Ruth.'

'Yes,' Ruth replied.

It was raining hard when they left. They stood in a shop doorway and as Ruth retrieved her umbrella from her bag, Dan tottered towards her. It wasn't clear whether he'd lost his balance or if he was lunging for a kiss. She swivelled her body round and tried to shake out the folded spokes of the umbrella. Her elbow stuck in his stomach and she felt its softness and vulnerability. She could see his reflection in the glass door. His hands dangled foolishly and he stuffed them in his pockets.

She felt a rush of pity and when she turned back she gave him the umbrella.

'Because you're taller.' She took his arm and steadied him as they walked home.

In her living room they sat in armchairs either side of the fire, listening to the put put of the gas, drinking tea.

He said, 'I'm sorry I drank so much, Ruth. I suppose I was nervous.'

'Nervous of me?'

'After not seeing you for so long.'

She shifted her eyes away from his. She felt the sweat break out on the back of her neck.

'Is that Alice?' he asked. 'I thought she was older.'

'She is.' Ruth said. She had lots of recent photos of Alice, but she preferred to keep the one of her at eight years old on the mantelpiece. She loved the openness of her face.

Dan pulled a yellow packet from his jacket. 'Here.'

Ruth studied the pictures of his children. The girls grinned toothily at the camera, squinting in the sun's glare. The boy looked just like the young Dan.

'Love is not love
Which alters when it alteration finds.'

That was the sonnet Dan had recited to her in the transport café. She remembered now the reisty smell of the bacon and the two lorry drivers in the corner laughing at them.

Dan's son looked up at her. His expression was slightly flirtatious, sardonic and a bit sulky. Just like his father. Tears suddenly streaked her vision.

Dan was mesmerized by the flames of her gas fire. At last she looked at him properly. He was dishevelled and uncared for, but a woman would sort all that out. A new haircut and regular visits to the dry cleaner's and the gym and he would be handsome again. It wasn't that *he* had changed.

'Your wife wasn't there? On holiday?'

'D'you carry pictures of Tony to show people?'

She smiled. 'No.'

'I'd like to see a picture of Tony, actually.'

'Why?'

'To see what he's got that I haven't.'

'How d'you mean?' Her throat muscles tensed and her voice came out strangled.

Dan leaned over and took both her hands in his. 'He married the girl I should have married.'

His palms were dry as sand. She noticed that, unlike her, he was still wearing his wedding ring. He followed her eyes.

'I don't know why she left me. One day she said she'd just had enough. Out of the blue.'

'Yes,' she said.

'Then I realized we'd never been happy. It had never been right.'

'No,' she said.

He laced his fingers into hers 'It would have been all right between us, wouldn't it? Ruthie?'

She remembered how they used to slot their hands together like this in the transport café, on the bus and in the wings, waiting to go on stage. 'Maybe.'

But now his grip was too tight. And his eyes, which she had always thought were so beautiful, were too big in his face, which had become craggy.

She imagined them together in restaurants, on holiday, in bed. He would order the meals, book the hotels, lecture her and then try to please her. Their children wouldn't get on.

She stood up.

'I think I'll get off to bed. Red wine makes me sleepy. There's a bed made up in the spare room.'

He turned away from her.

'OK, Dan? Good night.' His shoulders were hunched. 'Sorry' was all she could think of saying.

Ruthie would have held him and comforted him. Listened to the story of his marriage until dawn. And slept with him when she was too tired to decide whether she wanted to or not.

Ruth, however, went upstairs to her own room and folded her clothes and put her best shoes in the drawer with gold handles beneath her bed. She took her makeup off carefully and rubbed night moisturizer into her skin. She dangled the red knickers like a twisted rope on the end of her painted toes before kicking them into the laundry basket.

She lay for a while with the light on, listening to Dan moving around her house. Living room. Stairs. Bathroom.

When at last she heard the spare room door click shut, she let herself cry. Quietly, so he couldn't hear.

Myra Connell

MYRA CONNELL grew up in Northern Ireland and now works in Birmingham as an Acupuncturist and Zero Balancer. She was a founder member of the writers' group Women & Words, and of Bleak House Books. Her 'mesmerizingly peculiar' stories and poems have been published in *Spinster*, *Writing Women* and *Her Majesty*.

Heidi's House

Myra Connell

Heidi's house in Springfield, Pennsylvania. July, 2002. It is silent, except for the whirr of the fridge. Then the single sound of the tap dripping into a bowl that I have left soaking in the sink.

It is eleven thirty a.m.

I have been sunbathing. I turned round and straddled the chair to tan my back. I didn't want to lie on the grass: it is coarse and sparsely sown, with patches of bare, baked earth, and ants scuttling between the blades. I considered lying on the table, which is made of hardwood, and invitingly smooth to the touch; but these silent houses all around might only seem to be empty, and I was put off by the thought that I might be observed.

Heidi's house is in a suburb. The streets are named after the states of America: Delaware, Pennsylvania, Maryland. The sidewalks have grass on both sides and tall trees shading them, so that walking here is like walking in the woods. The houses are detached, with large gardens and no fences. Many of them have patriotic arrangements of flags in the front, and slogans painted on boards: 'Welcome'; 'God Bless America'; 'In God We Trust'.

It is too hot to sit out any longer and so I have come inside. The lino feels sticky and I walk on the outside edges of my feet so as to touch it as little as possible.

I sit down at the table in the dining room, facing the archway into the kitchen. I have checked, looked everywhere like a dog searching for a place to lie down, and this is the best place in the house to work. Even so, I don't feel comfortable. I would like to have a table in front of a sunny window; but there is nothing like that here, and nothing I can do to produce it. Moving furniture would be taking too much of a liberty; and in any case, everything is designed to keep the sun out. Some of the windows are covered with blinds, and the house is shaded all round by the dense foliage of the trees.

At least from this spot I can see into the kitchen, which is bright. The sun is beginning to go off it now, but it is still touching the sink, glinting on the silver taps, and picking out highlights of blue: a glass on the drying rack, the washing-up liquid, a ladle hanging on the side of the cupboard. Plants grow on each side of the window. On the left a mother-in-law's tongue; on the right a scented geranium which has burgeoned so much over the summer that it is now draped over the tap: precariously balanced, the pot too light to keep it stable.

A fish, a black one with long waving fins and tail, lives in a bowl on the draining board. My job, my rent, as Angela tells me – breathless Angela with the shocking blue eyes and the five children and the trim body – is to feed him. It was Angela who let us in for our stay, bringing with her a huge basket of food: soup, a mushroom quiche, an immense salad of black grapes and three different kinds of melon. Mostly the fish hides under the fake rock in the middle of his home; but in the mornings when I come down, he emerges and waits expectantly, mouth to the surface, for his breakfast. I open the plastic lid of the container that holds his food, releasing a dry smell of fish. I have taken a teaspoon out of the drawer and I keep it by his bowl for removing anything that he hasn't eaten from the day before. I am supposed to do that. Also, only to give him three or four pellets a day. Even so, some uneaten morsels sink to the bottom. I know I shouldn't let this happen; but sometimes when I drop the pellets onto the surface the meniscus breaks and then they fall, and in the few days that I am here the water becomes progressively more foul. It has bubbles on the surface as if things are fermenting, and I hope that Heidi will be back soon, because I don't know what to do about this.

On the ceiling in the kitchen there is a patch of light, reflected from the bowl of water in the sink. When a drop falls in, it shivers and dances.

Heidi is Finnish.

Her furniture is painted in matt emulsion: a soft red, a faded and distressed green, several pieces in Ikea blue. The rooms are random and profuse, with paintings on the walls and through the arch a folksy print that shows happy children tripping along in a procession, with hobby horses and balloons. The girls wear loose smocks and pointy caps, the boys too-short trousers; and the ground under their dancing feet is a profusion of flowers.

Her husband is a painter.

Earlier, I dropped a mug into the sink. I had been wondering whether the sink was solid under its white enamel, or whether it was one of those flexible stainless steel ones: now I know that it is solid because the mug broke. The handle came off. I heard myself swearing. I felt the shock go through me. I noticed the quick thought: I hope Heidi knows we are here.

At midday the quietness in the house takes on an immanence, as if gathering in readiness for something. I can hear a clock ticking, with the dull unresonant tock of cheap plastic.

I move and sit on the last of the three steps that lead from the corner landing to the upper floor of the house.

They are carpeted in soft beige wool, entirely free of marks. Elsewhere the floors are of expensive parquet: close-grained wood laid immaculately in narrow strips and stained a reddish brown. But whoever painted the house – white all through – did it carelessly, and dripped paint all over these floors. In the corner of the living room they knocked over the paint tin. Maybe they were expecting the parquet to be sanded down and revarnished. Maybe Heidi doesn't care about white flecks on her floor. Or maybe the house is rented: some kid was paid a few dollars to give the place a quick coat between tenants, and by the time the spills were noticed Heidi was on her way from the airport and it was too late to do anything about them.

Across the landing is the study. There is a two-seater sofa in here, with a sheet loosely spread over it and a blanket thrown aside, as if someone had slept here the night before they left. And there is the terrarium, whose residents I also have to attend to. Glancing into it you just see vegetation and a pool of water. But if you look carefully, you will see a yellow lizard. He is usually upside down on the underside of the mesh lid of the tank. In the morning I have to switch on the light that shines in, and spray water; in the evening, switch off the light and spray again. In the mornings, I see the frog too. He is a shapely, chunky frog, smaller and stockier than the ones that live in my garden at home; and each day when I put the light on, he startles as if from a dream and stirs himself to crawl out of the pool. I don't have to feed them; there is a bowl of insects for their food.

Above me on the wall is a collection of family photographs. There are family photographs all over the house, but they are gathered, as if on a shrine, on these two walls facing each other across the stairs. Several show Heidi at her wedding: she wears a short salmon-pink shift dress in a heavy brocade. It has a high neck and long sleeves, and it doesn't suit her. She looks ungainly, and the dress seems an odd choice; but in another picture it is clear, from the way he has his hand on her belly and she looks up at him so proudly, that she was pregnant at her wedding. In all of these photos she looks outrageously happy, she smiles and smiles and smiles. She stands in the street with her husband's arm around her shoulders, and a group of younger men, drinking beer out of a bottle and laughing. She leans, in a pair of shorts with a white hat over her eyes, against the railing of a ship, and smiles. She smiles at another wedding, next to a bride in a long dress with stunning neckline and carrying a huge and beautiful bouquet. This bride is graceful, and turns her neck to dazzle the photographer, and I wonder how Heidi feels beside her ravishing sister; if she succumbs to the plainer woman's self-doubt, or if she knows that loving and being loved is what counts, not looking beautiful.

She certainly is loved. She is the queen in this house of men, attended by all of them. 'Benni for Mama' is written in crayon on a child's drawing stuck to the fridge. Next to it is another picture with the legend 'Axel loves Mama'. Above the desk a photo, mounted on a piece of yellow card, shows the two boys and their father snuggled under a duvet patterned with bold stars and stripes. One of the children has written across the top in purple, 'Happy Birthday Mama Heidi.' And her husband's portrait of her faces you eye-to-eye as you come down the stairs. Every time I pass it, I see her not-beauty, her not-stylishness; and the light in her eyes and the love with which he has painted her.

I am deep in the heat of the house, but the wall I am leaning against is chilly and I put a blanket over my shoulders. The light intensifies a little, and dims again as clouds move over the sun; subtly, without sharp edges.

Crickets are beginning to chirrup. A car drives by. I would like to sleep, but I am afraid that if I do, I will never be clear and focused again. I am afraid of the cold of the sheets.

Two o'clock. I sat there so that I could look again at the photos. There was one, of three little boys. All naked. All with white-blond hair. All with chubby legs. The oldest maybe six, the youngest one-and-a-half or two. They are standing in a green garden, eating doughnuts and smiling. It is a striking image, the three heads of almost-white silky hair, and the three little bodies and the three stubby penises, too short to hang, too babyish to jut much. I saw this and I thought Heidi had three sons. And yet elsewhere there are only two: two bunks in the long bedroom at the front of the house; two desks, each with its chair and its pot of coloured pens; two pairs of wellington boots in the back porch, two raincoats hanging above them.

And so I wonder if there had been another child. Whether something happened to him, and the two others lost their brother. Whether this is the story behind the huge painting by Heidi's husband that hangs at the foot of the stairs and dominates the living room. It depicts two figures – archetypal figures, larger than life – in grief. The man, a patriarch, with greying hair and broken eyes, leans in to the viewer. One massive sinewy hand is covering his mouth, the fingers twisted deep in the hairs of the beard. The face is creased. The hand pushing the skin makes a pouch under the eye. Behind him a woman, much younger, looks downwards in even more profound grief. She has a fine clear jawline, and wisps of her hair trail out from a loose tie. Her mouth is painted clumsily, so that it looks as if she has a black moustache; but this only emphasizes the sorrow on her face.

The days pass. I work. I feed the fish. I spray the frog and the lizard. The sun shines and the house is dark.

On the last day I clean up after us, and that is when I find out.

There is a bucket in the kitchen with cleaning equipment: bottles of stuff for floors and surfaces; cloths and rubber gloves; a nearly empty bag of wet wipes, carefully folded over so they won't dry out. But I can't find a mop or a hoover.

So I open the other door that leads from the kitchen. A flight of wooden steps goes down into a cellar. The lighting is good and the steps are sound. Children's board games are tidily stacked on shelves at eye level. The cellar is dry and spacious and well maintained, and it smells cleanly of washing powder.

A table-tennis table stands at the back, with several sit-on toys. Nearby is a washing machine and a tumble-drier and an ironing board. There is no mop, but in the corner at the bottom of the stairs two mattresses lean against a pillar making an enclosed place and behind them I see the curved top of the hose of a vacuum cleaner. I have to slide the mattresses back to reach it and as I lift it out I see it: a thing from a fairy story: a box, a wooden casket, the kind that we used to bury the ashes of my mother. It has brass handles and a plaque on the lid. I rest the hoover on the ground, balancing it with my hand, and I bend down to read the inscription. It says: *Kristian Johannsen. 1997–2001.*

I stand there for a moment. Maybe two. My heart is doing strange things, turning over like a porpoise in my chest. I wish I hadn't been mean about Heidi in her wedding dress. I wish I hadn't seen this. I can't understand why it is here, in the cellar, hidden away.

I don't touch it.

I take the hoover up the steps into the kitchen and then to the first floor. It is old and dirty and half-broken. It blows dust out as fast as it sucks it up, but I push it round the floors. I clean the bath, the basin, the toilet.

I strip the bed and put the used linen in a pile with the towels.

I start to take the sheet off the sofa in the study to straighten it, but I find potato chip crumbs in the creases. I imagine the father sitting here with his boys at bedtime, reading to them while they eat crisps. Three boys and then two. I wish I hadn't thought anything scathing about Heidi and her place, I wish I had been more respectful of her. I put the sheet back as it was, leaving the crumbs, and then I clean the lower rooms. Things look brighter, and I return the hoover to the cellar, replacing it in the corner behind the mattresses without disturbing the box.

When I've finished I put the broken mug in an out-of-the-way corner of the kitchen with ten dollars under it and a note saying *Sorry!* On the dining-room table I set another note thanking Heidi for letting us stay in her house. I weight it with a bottle of wine and we leave.

About what I found, I say nothing.

Hero

Myra Connell

H*e comes home more exhausted than it's possible for a man to be and still carry on living. His face is lined, covered with dust and streaked with sweat. These fall days have been clear and sunny, temperatures right up in the seventies many times; and anyway it's hot work, clearing rubble; and hurting work, not knowing what you'll find in it. It smells bad, and though you don't want to believe it, the fact is it smells bad with the rotting of the bodies that are in there. Smashed up; blasted into little pieces, many of them too small to be seen let alone put together into any-thing resembling a person. A few days it rained, and the water speeded up the rotting, and now the warmth again.*

He's in there, Simon, doing his bit; my son. He's lucky to be doing it: he's the only one alive from his engine. The bodies of two of them were found, their funerals were yes-terday. The others are still in there. They were the ones, Simon too, who were running up the stairs when everyone else was coming down, thinking they could put out that fire. They didn't see that it was impossible. It was too big, too high. But that's what they do, they put out fires; and they weren't going to stand there looking at it and waiting to see what would happen.

He was buried too. Thirty-six hours he was missing, and we thought he had to be dead. I went and stood with the others who had lost relatives. People brought us coffee and food, and at night they encouraged us to go back home and rest, and eventually I did go home. But not to rest. You don't rest when your own son is in something like that. I got through the night, and at dawn I went back and stood in the street as near as I could get to it, and just waited there with the other mothers and sweethearts and brothers and sisters and all. I pray to God I never have to live through another thirty-six hours like those.

By a miracle they heard him, and they dug him out with nothing more to see than some bruises.

Not the others though. They are still gone, and that was why he insisted on going back in there. He could have had time off, and he did take a couple of days. He came and stayed with me so as I could cook for him and take care of him. But he couldn't rest, he said he had to go back in and search for them.

He's over there every day now. They work six hours, then they have a break, then another six hours and they come home.

And then he'll take a can of beer out of the refrigerator and he'll sit down in front of the TV and he'll stay there all evening with his legs splayed out, slumped in the chair, drinking beer after beer till he falls asleep. The first few nights, I tried to wake him. 'Simon,' I said. 'You'd be better in bed, don't stay down here.' But he just grunted and told me to leave him be, and so I went upstairs. And that's how it's been most nights, and mostly I'll be sleeping at two or three in the morning and I'll hear him flush the toilet and then I'll be awake an hour, two hours, thinking about it all and worrying about him. I try not to worry, I know there's no sense in it and it only leaves me as exhausted as him in the morning. But that's how it is with worry, you'd turn it off if you could – but you can't.

It's silent in my head. I know there must be noise out there, because the things I am seeing are things that make noise. There are diggers, grabbing up rubble and tipping it into trucks. The engines make a noise, which grows louder when their power is being used to lift stuff. It is loud when the load is dropped into the trucks, the lumps of concrete tumbling in. Especially when the truck is empty, there is that hollow sound that rubble makes when it lands on steel. There are cranes too – they're quieter, but they're not silent – shifting girders and joists, carefully like pick-up sticks.

But I don't hear it. I don't hear the voices of the other men, either. We are all in shock. Most of us have stopped sleeping. We go to bed and all we see are images of what happened. The call on that sunny morning to the tower, and getting there and running in against the thousands of people who were running out. They gave us bottles of water on the stairs, and wished us luck. Nobody knew that the tower would sink down on itself the way it did, one floor on top of another till it was like a pile of pancakes, or that there was no way on earth that we could put out that fire, fuelled as it was by ten thousand gallons of jet fuel. And then the rubble falling and the hours in the dark underneath it, trying to keep calling out in spite of thinking, *This is how it ends for me*. The heat and the thirst and the fear, stuck in a space no bigger than a coffin which would collapse and let me be crushed if the beams holding it up gave way. And then the euphoria when I heard a far-away voice answer my shouting: the sudden miraculous ray of sunlight, and the sweetness of the air when they got to me, and the shock of the light as they dragged me out, breathing and uninjured. It just plays over and over.

We work close together, hand over hand, listening for signs that anyone else is alive under the heap. The trucks take the debris to the landfill site on Staten Island that's been re-opened on purpose for this job. Fresh Kills, it's called.

Over there, they sift through the stuff again for items that might be part of a person: watches, or credit cards; or body parts, of course. Each part has to have a separate bag, the same at the site. Thousands of body bags were delivered the first few days and people were appalled, thinking, Do they expect that many dead? They calmed down a bit when they realized. You can't have pieces of different people jumbled together in one bag. But there are thousands dead.

I don't want to send parts of human beings off in those trucks. It's important. I sift thoroughly, so it's just the rubble that goes. I work slowly, shifting it from one pile to another, checking, one lump at a time. I'm like an archaeologist digging with a spoon, so carefully. I shift a lump of stuff. I look underneath. I shift another lump. Sometimes I find things, and then I have to call the supervisor, and one of the other guys comes over with the bag and in it goes.

The first days, we were working shoulder-to-shoulder, there were so many people searching. For survivors then.

Now it's eased. Most people have given up expecting to find anyone else alive. Not everyone, though. There's Martin Seguard's wife. She comes to the firehouse with her daughter and the new baby. She brings photographs of Martin, and I show her others that we have, that were on the noticeboards and then taken down and kept. Martin at a Thanksgiving dinner. Martin standing on a stage making a speech. Martin singing. Martin always wearing the same tie. God is good, she says. God can create miracles, and we have to expect miracles not be surprised by them. 'I am expecting the miracle,' she says.

But the mayor has declared officially that it's not a rescue operation any more, it's a recovery operation. That means the best we can hope for is to find bodies. That's how it is. In reality, we're lucky to find recognizable parts of bodies, let alone parts that could be identified without DNA testing as belonging to a particular human being.

What have I found? A lot of stuff. A briefcase one day. I opened it to look inside. There was a lunch box; in it, all clean and pristine, you could see the sandwiches and a yogurt and a green apple. Someone going to be too busy to send down for food; or saving pennies; or maybe a health freak, wanting to know exactly what went into his system. It was a he. A man's umbrella. Papers. At first you look out of curiosity, though we're not supposed to. Then you become more used to it and you give up.

I found a shoe, the same style and the same soft pink colour that Marcie used to wear with summer dresses. It was that sort of day when it happened. September, but still warm. Just a week or so past Labor Day, when the life-guards have left the beach and the kids are back at school.

It was this time a year ago that Marcie told me she was expecting. We'd been to Coney Island for the day. She used to love it there and we were peaceful as we always were on the way back, sitting in the train, full with the sun and the wind and the sight of the ocean. Just as the train came out of the subway to go over the bridge onto Manhattan Island, she told me, and her face was lit up with happiness as well as with the sun. But I couldn't do it. I had to tell her, it wasn't what I wanted, not yet; it was too soon, we hadn't known each other long enough; I wasn't sure about her, or about her and me.

That was the end of us. She insisted on keeping the baby, and I insisted that I wasn't going to be steamrolled into settling down and getting married, and we couldn't straighten it out and so we went our separate ways. I felt bad, leaving her to raise the kid alone; but there was something in me that was stronger than that, that wouldn't keep quiet and I wouldn't shut it up.

*

Just the one shoe, all dusty, and squashed by the weight of stuff on top of it – though we're working high up on the ruins and this weight is nothing compared to the weight lower down. The pile is hundreds of feet high, a small mountain, and it goes deeper than the ground, because there were basements and the subway. I try to imagine the suffocation of being under that weight of matter, but I can't, it's impossible.

In the times before they found him, when I was home supposedly resting, I stood in front of the TV and watched it all. It was surreal, seeing over and over the image of the plane flying into the tower. It meant nothing, the mind couldn't grasp it. And then the sight of people tumbling from a window splayed and slowly falling, light figures against the dark ground of the towers' concrete. It's not weird, jumping out of a window on the fiftieth floor or the eightieth. It's instinct. When the heat is that intense and you're that close to being burned alive, you go anywhere to escape. They think more than three thousand people died. Thirty-five hundred they're saying today.

And then I found an arm. I jumped back when I touched it. Something that was once living, even if it's dead now, feels different, and the effect it had on me was like when I was a kid and I'd go out in my uncle's garden in Pennsylvania and help him, and sometimes I'd touch a slug hidden under the leaves. It can't hurt you, but you jump. I picked the arm up without seeing what it was and then I dropped it in disgust. Flesh. It has that spongy, rubbery feel. It was a woman's arm, the left arm, just the lower part of it. It had a bracelet on the wrist, a narrow gold chain with a couple of charms hanging from it. There was a ring on the finger, an engagement ring I suppose it would be. It had fallen palm down and I could see the two small diamonds on the ring. The nails had been painted, not loud and bright, but gentle, just a shine, and the whole thing all dirty and scratched and bloodstained now.

Once I'd got over the revulsion, I picked it up again and held it in my hands for a moment. We're not supposed to do that, not pause or think about what we're doing. It's just a job, they say. Not that they don't try to understand the things we go through. They have disaster counsellors come and talk to us, because they know that we might be traumatized by the work. It was the counsellor who said, the first week, 'Don't think too much about what you're doing. Your sanity depends on you knowing it's just a job. Keep that in mind while you're working. You're professionals. This is your job.'

But I found myself holding this girl's arm and looking at it.

I hope the weather cools down soon, it's too much, all this warmth in the fall. There are flies about, lots of them, we need the cold to kill the bacteria. Hard frost. Nothing smells bad in a frost.

The arm smelled. I started gagging, and I had to stop myself throwing up. It was beginning to rot at the severed end, and the fingers were swollen and discoloured. I saw the supervisor coming, he would notice if I was standing still. I wanted to lay the arm gently somewhere, but you have to watch how you move if you're just doing your job, you do it briskly. You don't do anything tenderly and reverently. So I got brisk. But I did lay the arm in a hollow between two lumps of concrete and then I covered it with another so that it had its own little coffin-shaped room.

'Everything OK, Dyer?' he said.

'Fine sir. Just taking a breather.'
'OK. Keep it up. Take a break at noon.'
'Sir.'

Even before this, he was different, Simon. He wasn't like his brother, straightforward, always knew he wanted to follow his dad into the service. Michael's fine, he's settled down, they've got a couple of kids, they come over and stay. Simon, though, he wasn't so sure. His father used to tell him, it's no good going into it half-heartedly, it's yes or no, there's no maybe, and he truly didn't put pressure on him, not on purpose at least. But one day when he was about to graduate from high school, Simon came home and said he'd decided, and that was that. I think he was exasperated with himself for wavering and he just plumped for one thing so as to be settled. And he stuck with it, he did a good job. Just didn't mix a lot, didn't spend more time over there than he had to, and sometimes in bed at night his father would tell me he worried about him. Before he died, he told me to watch out for Simon. He said, everyone needs support in that work, and you can't do it alone. But I have always felt that Simon was straining, that the job was a struggle for him in a way that it hadn't been for his father and wasn't for his brother.

I carry on shifting stuff till I can see the supervisor way over on the other side of our section, and then I go back to where I left the arm. I pick it up again, hunkering down close to the ground and keeping my back to the other men. One of the charms on the bracelet is a locket shaped like a heart, with a tiny keyhole and an even tinier sliding cover

over the hole. There's a key hanging there too on the bracelet, but it isn't the key to the lock on the heart, it's bigger. I
tug at the bracelet, moving it round on the arm till the clasp
is uppermost. My hands are stiff with the work; they're
like my uncle's hands, like hams my aunt used to say, and
my fingers are clumsy, way too big for this little fastening.
It's a tiny gold circle with a sliding knob no bigger than a
grain of coarse sand. After several attempts, I manage to
move the knob by catching it under the end of my nail, and
the opposing little circle slips out.

'OK, Simon, take a break.'

The supervisor's back. I hide the chain in my glove and
then instead of telling him I've found a body part, I return
the arm to its hiding place. I look round for something I
can use to mark the spot, but there isn't anything, so I just
leave it.

*He has dust all over him when he gets back. He doesn't stay
around at the end of the day to shower, he just gets out and
comes home.*

*But he doesn't speak. He's like they are as teenagers, on
the edge of something all the time and you can't say a
word to them because they'll bite your head off. The same
way that a teenage boy has of being in a world of his own,
somewhere you can't reach him.*

*I wash his clothes, and I clean the bathtub of the grit
that comes out of his hair. It gets everywhere, even in the
rubber lip of the front-loader, the place where the nickels
collect and the bits of gum wrapper that I miss in the
pockets of things. There's a puddle of water and grit.*

'Don't leave me,' I weep. 'Don't leave me.'

I'm cold and my chest hurts. Marcie isn't here, no one is here, it's just me in the bed with the sheets tangled. It's still dark outside.

I get up. I know how exhausted I am, I can feel the ache in the eyes and the weariness in the limbs. But the ache in my heart when I stay in bed is worse. I can't stand it.

I check the bedside clock. It's three a.m. If I leave now, I can get over there and be back for when the shift starts, as long as the lines on the bridge aren't too long. It's the way back that'll take the time, they're searching every vehicle now. I can't work it out, the timing. I try briefly but I'm not thinking clearly. I pull on my work clothes, put the boots on outside the door, get in the car and drive off.

Marcie doesn't answer the first few rings on the bell, but eventually she comes down.

'Who is this?' she calls.

'Marcie, open up, it's Simon.'

She opens the door but stands blocking it.

'Marcie . . .' I want to fall into her arms. I want it to be like it used to be, for her to take me upstairs with her. I want to feel her skin on mine and to bury my face in her breasts. I can feel the place on the top of my head that needs to be covered with her body: I need her cheek there, and her arms and legs wrapped around me.

She pulls her robe more closely round her.

I am ashamed. I am ashamed that I have come over here in the night needing her. I am ashamed that I didn't stick with her when the baby was on the way. I am ashamed that I was put off by the thought of all the days and days we would have to live through, the mundane and the routine and the dreary, being part of the family and staying the same for ever. All the energy that brought me here drains away. I feel desolate and cold and empty. I don't know how I'll get back, how I'll face the day.

'I . . . I . . . wanted to see you.'

'Oh yeah? So you came and woke me up at three a.m.? Terrific.'

'Marcie . . .' But her eyes are cold. She hasn't forgiven me. I turn and walk away.

I get back early, I have time to order eggs before work in Starkey's diner, and I eat a few mouthfuls.

This morning when I get up he has already gone.

I go out to buy groceries. It's still warm, and the leaves on the trees in the park are just beginning to change colour. Still a lot of green in with the golden ones, no frost yet to turn them, and the sun coming through, it's pretty. Over by the firehouse there's the shrine in memory of the men who are lost. A five-foot cross made of flowers, a statue of Our Lady. Bunches of flowers laid against the fence, still wrapped in cellophane from the shop. Candles on the sidewalk, and messages: letters from kids to their fathers who have gone, letters from girlfriends to boyfriends, prayers from ordinary people moved by what has happened. There's a big banner that some schoolkids made in Madison, Wisconsin. The teacher got this big piece of cloth and the kids drew themselves, whole body, all carrying the stars and stripes in their right hand, so there's a big circle of figures, each with the name underneath. Third graders I'd say from the writing and drawing, and one of them has written his name huge, and in the middle it says, WE LOVE YOU *and* GOD BLESS AMERICA.

I buy a chicken for dinner, to make him something he likes. He needs to eat, he has lost weight. And aged. There are deep lines on his face that were never there before.

I go on with the work. I try to do as the other guys do and just wave the stuff into the trucks, and if I come across anything, put it in a bag. Midway through the morning, close to where I found the arm, I find something else. It's one of those cute purses that young women carry, with a thin strap that goes over one shoulder and across the body. It has fancy edges to the flap and a gold clasp. This time I don't hesitate, I just glance round quickly to see that no one's watching me and I put it straight into my pocket, then carry on working.

I set out to walk after the shift. It's dark. I walk over to the Hudson, to the Battery Park walkway.

It is still nice over here. The ferry going over to Staten Island. The lights on a building opposite change color, purple and red and yellow, slowly shifting so that if you look away for a minute, when you look back they have changed without you seeing it happen. People are still out, walking and jogging and skating. But everything has sobered up. The things that seemed fun before, the things that people chased hoping they would make them happy, the gadgets and the pretty clothes and the brand-name trainers, and the shows and the bars and the ball games, all that no longer seems to matter. We were playing, engrossed and oblivious, and now the world is a different place and we are stopped in our tracks and not sure what is true. It's like when the teacher was late for class. Us kids would go wild: someone would be spraying potato chips, someone else would be dancing on the table, and another guy would be red faced with excitement at putting tennis balls down his sweater to look like a pair of tits. And then the teacher would walk in and suddenly everyone would be frozen and sheepish and embarrassed, caught in the act. There's a silence hanging over the city and down here there's less life than there used to be. The lights are still on and the water still sparkles and the wind turbines on the dredging platform still turn away making their little sound; but there are fewer people about, and they are subdued. The Mayor, he wants everyone to live as normal; he says that giving up the regular things is giving in to the terrorists. He talks about the spirit of New Yorkers, and how we won't be beat by any of this. But ordering it can't make it happen.

I sit on a bench facing the railing and the river. After a bit I take the purse out of my pocket, and hold it in my hand. I wonder about the girl who wore it, and I think about the guys who are dead. But not clearly, and somehow not *enough*. It's too much to take in. I don't know if I'll ever understand it, that they're gone. I'm at a door in my mind and behind the door is the understanding and the knowledge and the grasping that they're not here any more. I know that if I could get the door to open I would comprehend. But I can't.

By and by I open the purse. Inside are three compartments, the central one with a zipper. I bring things out and lay them on the seat beside me: a lipstick and a comb; a pen; and a hinged makeup case with pink powder and a brush and a mirror. In the zippered compartment I find her wallet and a bunch of keys. There's some money in the wallet, a couple of bank cards, and an ID with a tiny photo: a blonde girl, straight hair drawn loosely back, nothing exceptional about her, and her signature, 'Theresa Kandarowski' neat and unpretentious. There are a couple of receipts from Macy's, and one from Century 21; and then a letter:

> I want you to have this. It's to go with the ring. The key
> to my heart! I love you, see you tonight. Don.

The envelope has her address on it. She's done what everybody knows not to do, carried her keys with her address in the same place.

I get up and walk again. I walk all along the Battery, right to the end and then I turn round and come back. Everything is dissolving. There's nothing left to hold onto.

I should go back home and sleep. But it's no good. The place where I have to be is the site, I need to go back there.

The cop at the gate is an older man; tall and solid, his belly hanging over his belt.

'Officer, I left my wallet inside, I need to get back in.'

'You wanna go in?'

'I do.'

He looks me up and down. 'You'll never find your wallet in there. You've lost it, buddy.'

'I need to check. Sentimental value.'

'You got a pass?'

I show him my ID.

'Well, it's irregular.' He looks at me, his eyes narrowed, his head tilted back. I stand there, waiting. 'You lost your wallet?'

I know he knows that's not true. He can see I'm about spent and he seems to decide that some things are more important than the rules.

He unlocks the gate. 'You take it easy, buddy. Nothing has more value than your life.' He pushes the gate open with his arm. 'Here,' he says, 'take this.' He's holding something out to me. It's a silver hip flask. 'You look like you could use it.'

The flask is old, polished, and warm from his pocket. 'Thanks.'

Part of the working area has been taped off since this morning. The lights aren't on there; it's dark, darker than anywhere in the city ever was at night, because the buildings all around that used to have lights blazing at nearly every window even when they were empty, are deserted, out of bounds until all the checks have been run on their safety. The area to the left is violently illuminated by rows of arc lights. When I look away from them, the blackness here becomes even thicker. I have to stop and stand still for several seconds till my eyes get more used to it, and even then I stumble on the rough ground.

I think that if I could find the girl's arm, that would be good. That's it, I'm looking for the girl's arm. And after that I'll look for the rest of her. It seems to me that if I could find the parts of her and put them back together, something useful would have been done. The whole lie of the place has changed, a lot of stuff has gone or been moved, but I clamber about until I judge by the angle and distance from the remnants of the tower that I've found the place. It's disorienting, the dark, and the bright light behind me, which blinds me again if I turn towards it.

I stand teetering on a pile which slides under me. When it stabilizes I take a few pulls from the flask. The whiskey makes a warm trail all the way down to my stomach. It sets my guts moving and I think I might have to shit. Then the warmth reaches my brain and I feel more cheerful. The arm should be here somewhere, and then I'll find the rest of her. She must be here, I'm sure of it. I start shifting rubble. But my sense of hope and purpose drains away in seconds. Without gloves the lumps of stuff are too big and solid, and my hands feel weak and fragile. I hurt my thumb picking something up awkwardly and I see that this is an impossible task.

I sit down heavily. Now that my purpose has gone, the ache in my heart gets so strong that I think I won't bear it. I want to weep, but I can't. I notice the silence in my head again. A man is working high up with an acetylene cutter, under a bank of lights on a tower like they have at the base-ball ground, and there's a crane with a rope and pulley. They're dismantling the remains of the metal frame of the building one piece at a time. Cut a section off. Lower it.

Take it away. Cut another section. Do it again. Laboriously, piece by piece.

When I come round, cold and stiff, it's dawn. I've slept, or passed out. My jacket and pants are damp with dew. The purse has fallen to the ground. I ache, it seems like I just can't move, not a muscle, not to bend a leg to stand up.

I pull myself together, it feels like literally, gathering all my strength and will power for the effort of moving. I pick up the purse and put it back in my pocket, then get to my feet and head for the gate. The guard is going off duty. 'Find what you were looking for, son?' he asks. I lurch past him without looking up or speaking.

Other men are coming in now with a morning briskness about them that I recognize from before. Maybe they generate it by being together, the way bits of dead metal banging together will make a spark.

I avoid them and start walking. If I have a destination it's Marcie's place, but nothing is clear in my mind. The streets are empty of the people who would usually be coming in for work now. Instead there are vehicles carrying rescue workers. Men are already working on the road: they've dug it up to get to the pipes and cables underneath. There are arc lights here too, going off, and a wooden boardwalk has been built beside the excavations with a painted railing to keep people from stepping into the trench. A little further on, I buy coffee from a stall and lean against a wall to drink it. I eat a few bites of a doughnut. The sun's shining, but the air is still cool after the night, and the steam rises white from the coffee. Children go with their moms, hand in hand, off to school. Across the street is one of the shrines to dead people, photos stuck to the railings; and when I've eaten and drunk all I want, I go and check them out. Not firefighters these, but people who worked in the towers as janitors and office workers, secretaries, clerks; ordinary folks who came into this part of town for their jobs.

I wouldn't have recognized her from the photo, but when I've spotted the name, I see it is her. The same girl, Theresa Kandarowski, there's her face, she's sitting at a table in a restaurant with a group of friends, someone has circled her head with a pen, and there's an address and a number to call.

I don't call it. Instead I check the address on the envelope in the purse. Park Place.

The apartment is in a new building, one of three. There are fancy restaurants opposite, but these places are subsidized, you can tell by the decor. It's easy to get past the doorman sitting behind his desk in the lobby. He hasn't noticed that security is supposed to be tight now. I take the elevator to the tenth floor. It's empty, and I use the privacy to fumble in her purse for the keys. I'm about to unlock the door when I remember that someone might be home. I ring the bell; but nobody answers, so I open the door and go in.

It's a nice place. There's a pale wooden floor. Plants in the corners, and a big one hanging in a basket fixed to the ceiling, its long, green and white striped leaves cascading like a fountain up and over and down. The furniture is new, and upholstered in dark blue with bright green cushions. In one corner there is a white table with four chairs, and a candle in a glass holder in the middle. There are long windows with curtains made of some gauzy stuff.

A French door opens onto a balcony and I go out. It looks right over the site, you can see the whole thing. The heap of wreckage. The empty buildings around, some of them with windows broken, one with a screen of red mesh covering it from roof to street so that falling debris can't cause injuries. I can see the men working, and the machinery, and the skeletons of the towers, and beyond is the

Hudson, sparkling in the sun. She had flowers on her balcony, Theresa, and now they're covered in fine white dust, and so is the chair she had out there for sunbathing, and the table next to it with the empty coffee cup from breakfast that day.

I don't know if I have a purpose here. I don't want to steal anything, or pry. A guy sneaking into a strange girl's apartment, could be weird or sick, but there's none of that in me.

I have made footprints in the dust on the balcony and when I go back in I see I've left tracks on the floor also. No one has come in to clean up, and I wonder if I would have done under the circumstances, if it had been my daughter or girlfriend who'd been lost. I don't know. Maybe. When they do come, they'll know someone has been here. Or maybe they won't, maybe they'll be too upset to notice, or more dust will have settled and hidden the signs of my visit.

Without having accomplished anything, I leave. All I've touched in the apartment are the two door handles and I wipe them with my sleeve as I go out. I feel heavy with a kind of dull despair. I hate myself. I hate that I am alive and the others are dead. I hate that I messed up with Marcie, and that I have a son who I hardly know. If I could go back to her I would, forgetting the reasons I had for resisting.

It's after four in the afternoon when I get outside again. I still have no plan. I cross the street to the railing with the photograph. I could call the number but it seems too difficult. I write down the address instead. It's a ways away, somewhere in New Jersey; but going there seems more possible than explaining myself over the phone.

*

When I arrive it's beginning to get dark.

The pointlessness of it all almost overwhelms me, and the inadequacy of what I am doing. People want their loved ones back, even if they fought with them that morning over breakfast, even if they were wondering about having an affair or actually embarking on one. They don't want what I am bringing.

It's a wood house with a yard, her parents' place. It all looks clean and well kept and I am aware that I am filthy. I smell, my breath smells, I am unshaven. I go up to the door. The bell sounds.

'Ma'am,' I say to the woman who answers. 'I found this.' I hold out the purse.

'Where did you find that?' she asks. She looks haggard and pale, blue circles under her eyes.

Where would she think I found it? In the street? Does she think maybe her daughter dropped it on her way to the store and she's going to be back in ten minutes?

'I found it on the site,' I say. 'The World Trade Center site. I found her arm too, I brought you this.' I offer her the bracelet. 'I shouldn't have taken it but I did.'

I am standing there holding them both out, the purse and the bracelet.

'They belonged to your daughter. I found them at the site. I found her arm.'

She didn't invite me in. She took the things. Later she will have official notification of her daughter's death. They will make a positive identification using DNA sampling.

That's the end of the story. I go home. I get sick leave, three months. No one else from the station is found.

When they say I'm well enough to work, I don't go back where I was. I close the book on that.

I take a job at a desk. Marcie has found someone else now. I don't see much of her, just at the door on alternate

Sundays when I go over to pick up Steven. We go to the movies or to the park and stop at McDonald's on the way home, and once in a while I take him on the ferry or out to Coney Island, trying to do like the Mayor said. But it's more or less just keeping going at present.

About the Editor

LESLEY GLAISTER – 'one of Britain's finest writers' – is the author of *Honour Thy Father*, which won the Somerset Maugham Award and a Betty Trask Award, and more recently *Easy Peasy*, *Sheer Blue Bliss* and *Now You See Me*. Her tenth novel, the menacing and engrossing *As Far as You Can Go*, was published by Bloomsbury in March 2004. Lesley teaches a Masters Degree in Writing at Sheffield Hallam University.